MW01688631

The kiss went deep and hard suddenly, both of them struggling for control. *Come on, Tank. Show me what you want.*

He got just what he wanted, TJ kissing him until he couldn't breathe. He dragged one hand down that broad chest, his palm open so he could feel Tank's heart race.

They drew back just enough to look at each other, TJ's blue eyes wide open now. Then they dove in again. Not so safe, was he?

This time it was Wacey who closed his eyes, his focus on those drugging kisses. This was real.

Welcome to

Dreamspun Desires

Dear Reader,

Love is the dream. It dazzles us, makes us stronger, and brings us to our knees. Dreamspun Desires tell stories of love featuring your favorite heartwarming heroes, captivating plots, and exotic locations. Stories that make your breath catch and your imagination soar.

In the pages of these wonderful love stories, readers can escape to a world where love conquers all, the tenderness of a first kiss sweeps you away, and your heart pounds at the sight of the one you love.

When you put it all together, you find romance in its truest form.

Love always finds a way.

Elizabeth North

Executive Director
Dreamspinner Press

BA Tortuga

COWBOY IN THE CROSSHAIRS

DREAMSPUN DESIRES

PUBLISHED BY

DREAMSPINNER PRESS

Published by
DREAMSPINNER PRESS

5032 Capital Circle SW, Suite 2, PMB# 279,
Tallahassee, FL 32305-7886 USA
www.dreamspinnerpress.com

This is a work of fiction. Names, characters, places, and incidents either are the product of author imagination or are used fictitiously, and any resemblance to actual persons, living or dead, business establishments, events, or locales is entirely coincidental.

Mass Market Paperback ISBN: 978-1-64108-035-4
Digital ISBN: 978-1-64080-036-6
Library of Congress Control Number: 2017911079
Mass Market Paperback published March 2018
v. 1.0

Printed in the United States of America
∞
This paper meets the requirements of
ANSI/NISO Z39.48-1992 (Permanence of Paper).

BA TORTUGA, Texan to the bone and an unrepentant Daddy's Girl, spends her days with her basset hounds, getting tattooed, texting her sisters, and eating Mexican food. When she's not doing that, she's writing. She spends her days off watching rodeo, knitting, and surfing Pinterest in the name of research. BA's personal saviors include her wife, Julia Talbot, her best friend, Sean Michael, and coffee. Lots of coffee. Really good coffee.

Having written everything from fist-fighting rednecks to hard-core cowboys to werewolves, BA does her damnedest to tell the stories of her heart, which was raised in Northeast Texas, but has heard the call of the high desert and lives in the Sandias. With books ranging from hard-hitting GLBT romance, to fiery ménages, to the most traditional of love stories, BA refuses to be pigeonholed by anyone but the voices in her head.

Website: www.batortuga.com
Blog: batortuga.blogspot.com
Facebook: www.facebook.com/batortuga
Twitter: @batortuga

By BA Tortuga

DREAMSPUN DESIRES

#6 – Trial by Fire
#30 – Two Cowboys and a Baby
#53 – Cowboy in the Crosshairs

LEANING N

#16 – Commitment Ranch
#42 – Finding Mr. Wright

Published by **DREAMSPINNER PRESS**
www.dreamspinnerpress.com

For my evil twin, Kiernan.
Love you, honey, more than my luggage.

Acknowledgments

MANY thanks to Jaymi and Jodi for their input and constant support.

Chapter One

"CHIEF! Chief Cook! Did you see how that insane woman, that Starbaby Flutterbeans or whatever she's calling herself this 'incarnation' painted her house? There's a nekkid lady on the side. A *naked* woman!" Ruth Ann Masters was just about to work herself into a right tizzy or a stroke—one of which would be funny as all get-out.

"Miz Masters, that's the Venus of Willendorf, and it's art. She ain't breaking no laws." Maybe a few of common decency, but that wasn't under his particular elected umbrella. Some droopy boobs and a wide belly wasn't exactly pornalicious.

"But it's naked! Think of the children."

"If you stay out of Star's yard, you can't see it." It was hidden by that giant pyracantha that shaded the house and the labyrinth that Star'd built out of yard art in her side yard.

"I was not in her yard!"

"Now, Miz Masters, you're yelling." Jenny, who owned the Turquoise Café, came to refill TJ's coffee. "Not dignified."

"Thank you, Jenny."

"Look here, you…. My people have been in this town since it was created. I'm—"

"A nosy old biddy?"

Oh Lord, just what he needed, Josh Leman stirring the shit pot.

TJ tried hard not to roll his eyes. "Josh, you hush. Miz Ruth, I can tell you the kids like it."

Josh plopped down beside him, his oldest and orneriest friend covered in dust. "What? You are a nosy one, Miz Ruth. You know I love you, but you need to leave Star alone."

"She's a witch!" the old lady screamed.

"That ain't illegal, honey. Come on, have a cup of tea on the house." Jenny rolled her eyes over Ruth's shoulder.

"That sounds good, huh? Get her a scone on me." He glared at Josh. "What the what, buddy? I don't need her writing an op piece to the newspaper."

"Oh, you know Mike would piss himself if he could have a little war." Josh was nowhere near worried enough.

"I do know. I also know what I'll get from the mayor, and Star would curse my dick or something."

"God forbid." Josh leaned back and grinned at him, gold front tooth glinting. "So, I come bearing gossip. Interested?"

"Fuck yes." He needed something besides the shit show of being a small-town cop.

"Okay. Normal stuff first. Diane Colley is having an affair with Jane Tees. Her husband caught them munching carpet last week. Matt Colley's getting the kids and the house; Diane's taking the pottery studio and every other weekend."

"Oh, ouch. I mean, for all of them." Diane was a neat lady but a bit of a flake. The kids would be better off with Matt, he thought.

"I know, right? I mean, Jane's a smart cookie. I hope she knows what she's getting into." Josh paused dramatically. "Pun intended."

"Ew." Josh could be hilariously crude. "That's not polite, bud."

"Like I do polite. What else.... Wacey Bene is coming back to town to stay with his folks at the ranch. He got hurt real bad in Cheyenne. Also, my Loretta caught pregnant."

"Wait, what?" He blinked, trying to process that.

"It's true. She's due right after Christmas."

TJ rolled his eyes. "No, doof. About Wacey. What happened?"

"Dunno. Something about the horses, I think."

No. No, that didn't make a lick of sense. Wacey Bene was a dick of the highest order, but the man had been born on horseback. He wouldn't get in any kind of accident with a horse.

"How bad is he hurt?"

"Did you not hear me? I am having a baby, you cocksucker."

"Hey! Congratulations." He grinned wide, knowing it made Josh nuts to be ignored. "Go you."

"I know, right? I thought it would never happen. She's over the moon."

"Are you sure it's yours? What if you're shooting blanks?"

"I will shoot you right here, fudge packer." Josh's smile never ever faltered. Everyone deserved that—to be loved and trusted without a bit of hesitation. Josh had married Loretta the day after high school graduation, had put her through college at UNM, and had built her the house of her dreams. Those two were disgusting in love.

He grinned. "I'll arrest you for trying. Seriously, man, congratulations. Kids will change your life forever."

TJ knew all about that. His boys were the light of his fucking life.

"Good. I would have been happy one way or the other, but my girl? She was getting plumb down in the mouth about not being able to catch."

"I know. When it's time, it's time. Jenny, give Josh another round of pancakes on me."

"I can do that." She nudged Josh's arm. "Congrats, man."

"Thank you."

"So, what were you asking about?" Josh murmured. "Oh! Wacey. He broke a leg or a hip or something. Bad enough that he's in a wheelchair for like another six weeks."

"Ouch." He winced, because that had to be hell for the kid and his folks, both.

Kid. Yeah, TJ reckoned Wacey wasn't a kid anymore, but he hadn't seen the jerk in ages.

Hell, damn near ten years, he guessed. Had it been that long since the oldest Bene son had been home? Surely not…. Then again, TJ would have heard about it if Wacey was around.

Josh grabbed the syrup. "Yep. Sucks to be him."

"I guess so." Christ, they'd been hot and heavy, once upon a time, but that was a different world, and he'd been a scared kid. No way they would have made it.

"You gonna eat that bacon?" Josh asked.

"Yes." He made a stabbing motion with his fork. "Back off."

"So, you got plans today besides sitting on your ass?"

"Yeah. I have a good bit to look into, actually." He had dick. Turquoise, New Mexico, was a tiny town with pretty tiny problems. Miz Ruth's complaint, which he wouldn't even research, was going to be the biggest deal of the day.

Josh gave him an exaggerated yawn. "Poor Chief."

"I know, I know. I'm overworked and underpaid." Hell, he loved his job, loved his kids, loved his life.

"You want one more round of pancakes for the road?"

"Heck yes." Why not? He would work it off.

"Good deal. I'm eating for two now, you know."

"I don't think that's exactly how it works."

"No?" Josh laughed loud and long. "Any excuse to eat. Jenny! Bring on another round."

"Lord have mercy. We should all have a hollow leg."

"Someday I'll be all paunch, but for now, I can shed it fast." Josh winked broadly.

Shit, as much as Josh was climbing up and down ladders, the man would never be chunky.

TJ waved Jenny over to pay the bill. This round he was going to have to eat and run, but he would suck down the butter and syrup any way he could. He had to pick his boys up after school today, not to mention all the paperwork at the office.

They powered through one more plate each. "Okay, Josh, I got to go. Keep an ear out about Wacey Bene." TJ could have bitten his tongue. Why did he say that?

"Will do." That was the sign of a good friend—when they knew when to just agree about the ex.

He left the tip on the table before rising. “Later, bud. See you on Friday, Jenny!”

“Stay safe, Chief,” she answered, just like always.

That was always the plan too. He had too much to live for to get caught flat-footed out there. Good thing Turquoise was probably the least dangerous town in New Mexico. Time to do his job and keep it that way.

Chapter Two

"BUBBA. Welcome home."

Wacey opened his eyes, casting his gaze on the Bene Ranch and Rodeo School for the first time since he was a teenager. The big old adobe hadn't changed a bit—from the ristras hanging on the porch to the canales that had Mama's roses planted underneath. "It looks the same."

"You're the one that changed, Bubba." Lacey was the oldest and the bossiest one of all of them, and that hadn't changed either. "This house has stood here for three generations. It's never going to change."

"I don't need the guilt, Lace. I've been working." He was hurting so bad he was thinking about cutting his legs off at the knees.

"I wasn't going for guilt. I was pointing out your general stupidity." She grinned at him, her near-black eyes glinting. "We've been in a car for two days since I picked you up from the hospital, and I haven't given you shit. Give me a break."

"I did. I'm way less work than the twins."

"The devil himself would be less work than those two demons."

Wacey had to laugh, even though he was considering death as a viable option. "So we should be feeling sorry for Macey?"

Lace shook her head. "Nah. She's got the six already. What's two more?"

"Yeah. Good thing y'all are doing that little job for me."

"Shit, Macey's repopulating the entire town. We'll feel sorry for Kacey, Bubba. He's trying to fill your boots out there, and he's scared." Lacey put the truck in Park. "Time to face the fam, bud."

"Are they all in there?"

"Mama, Pop, Pap-Pap, Ma-Maw, Mami, Papi, Macey, Tim, Derek, Auntie Flora and Uncle Bam, and—"

"Stop. Just stop. Wheel me out to the casita?" The folks were bad enough. All of them? Jesus, Mary, and Joseph.

"Coward." She gave a serious look, though. "I'll tell Mama to come down, okay? She's wanting to see you real bad."

"You know I won't do that. You're supposed to just take me in."

"Are all gay cowboys this complicated?"

"Most of us are worse."

She chuckled, but dutifully hopped out of the truck to grab his wheelchair, then came to help him wrangle into it.

Uncle Bam and Lace's husband, Derek, were out there before she could do anything.

"Dammit, woman! Let us lift him. You don't need to be doing that in your condition. Hey, Wacey. Welcome home, man." The safety man grinned at him, winked. "You survived my wife. Congrats."

"Condition? Are you knocked up again, Sister?"

"Shut up." She glared at all of them in turn. "I'm going to get cookies set out."

"Dude, you didn't tell me?"

"You had enough on your mind." She marched away up the walk.

"Congratulations, you turd!" he called after her, and Uncle Bam cracked up.

"You got her number. How you feel?"

"Hurtin'." That was the best he had.

"We'll get you on inside, and you can take a pill." Uncle Bam knew the score. He'd broken more bones than anyone Wacey knew.

Derek had him settled before he could think to hurt too. "Your mama made tamales and green chicken enchiladas and beans."

His belly snarled audibly, and Uncle Bam snorted. "Oh, you just made her year with that sound, Dub."

"I bet. I love Tex-Mex, but Mama makes the best tamales." He breathed deep, the air still crisp with the tail end of winter. He'd been staying down between Austin and Houston during his months off. There, spring started in February.

Here, it waited until May.

"Mama makes the best everything, hmm." And there she was—reaching out to him with hands laden with silver-and-turquoise rings, the touch the single most comforting thing he'd ever felt.

"Mama."

"Mijo." She kissed his forehead. "Come in. Come in. I told everyone to be quiet."

"It's okay. Just tired and hurtin' some." He let Derek wheel him all the way into the kitchen, wanting to sit where it was warm and familiar.

Everything in him relaxed in a rush, and he couldn't figure out why he'd stayed gone so long. The room was easily the size of his entire apartment in Austin—the big island tiled in Saltillo tiles, the whole place flooded with light.

He loved the bright blue tiles popping in the backsplash, his mama's herbs hanging from a drying rack back by the pantry. "Wow. It's good to be home."

"Good to have you here." Pop leaned against the counter, his father's bright red hair and freckled face wreathed in concern. "I talked to Kacey and had that entire remuda sold off, son. I can't risk this happening again."

"It wasn't them. There was a bang—a backfire or something. I told you that." By the time Kace heard the commotion, it was all over but the crying.

"I know. I also know we can't have a breeder on our rotation who has such skittish mares going out." Pop shrugged, reminding Wacey he was a businessman first. He loved the livestock, but unlike Wacey, they were not his life.

"Tell me they went somewhere good, Pop."

"Of course they did, mijo. Now you need to breathe and heal and have some tamales."

He glanced at Mama, but he waited for Pop to answer too.

"They went to the lady up in Taos who runs that mustang rescue. She'll adopt them out as companion horses," Pop said. "Macey handled it for us."

"Cool." Oh thank God. Macey loved horses as much as he did. Kace was into the bucking bulls.

"Don't think I don't know you don't trust me." Pop handed him a cup of… hot tea? When he raised a brow, Pop gave him a stern look. "Doc says coffee will make you queasy with your pills."

"Oh, good Lord…."

"Don't start, Dub. You know it won't do a bit of good." Derek looked like butter wouldn't melt in his mouth.

"Have you told them Lace is knocked up again?" he countered.

Pop and Mama both set up a hue and cry, and he could laugh, knowing he'd gotten the best part of the upper hand. Let Derek fight all that pent-up worry.

Him, he just leaned back and sucked in green-chile-flavored air.

Damn, it was good to be home.

Chapter Three

FRIDAY morning at the diner turned out to be a busy one. Josh wasn't there with TJ, but everyone on earth turned out to complain about their neighbor, and the kids had a long weekend, so Monica was dropping them off in a few minutes.

It was probably the most important part of his job, and he felt weirdly like a medieval king, hearing folks' worries while he drank coffee and listened to oldies country.

Jenny's wife, Betsy, was working today, singing along with Freddy Fender in Spanish on that last teardrop song. She was a round, pillowy lady who smelled like bacon grease and syrup. He adored her.

"Chief, is it true they're going to bring in a Chili's here? Right on Pima?" Martha Netter had her "No

Corruption in My Town" T-shirt on and an activist's twinkle in her eyes.

"No, ma'am. Why would a Chili's move out here?"

"I dunno. Alina Wineberger said she'd seen the plans."

"Well, I can assure you, no new restaurants have applied for any permits or rented property."

"Oh, excellent. I made ginger cookies. Want some?"

"I do." He would let the kids go crazy. Enough sugar this morning and they'd nap all afternoon.

She handed him a bag of cookies that were heavy as neutron stars.

Okay, maybe he would use them to grind up and make a pie crust. They might break a tooth or something if someone tried to eat them.

"Thank you, ma'am. How's your Howard?"

"Recovering, thanks. He appreciated the care package you sent."

"Good." Poor Howard had been through two surgeries in six months. It sucked.

She wandered off, letting him sip his coffee and get a refill.

The bell over the door jangled, and TJ glanced up, smiling when he saw his boys come tumbling through the portal.

"Boys!" He held his arms open, impatient for his sons—Thomas, six, and James, four—to reach him.

"Daddy!"

"Hey, guys! Have you been good for Momma?" He hugged when they lunged at him, smacking kisses on their heads.

"Yes, sir! We been real good." Tommy grinned at him, showing off the gap where a front tooth was growing in.

"Have they?" he asked, winking at his ex-wife when she walked in behind them.

"Yessir." She leaned down and kissed his cheek. "Hey, Mister. How's it going?"

"Not bad at all. You gonna stay and have pancakes?"

"Cancakes!" James bounced.

"I am, yeah. I need breakfast before I start my shift at the hospital."

"Excellent. Move in, you," he told Thomas, who scooted to let his mom in on one side of the booth while James stayed with him on the other.

"How's it going, you?" he asked, and she shot him a tired grin.

"Good. The boys are behaving. Mother's behaving. Work is behaving. A disaster should be right around the corner."

"No sh—kidding." He winked at her when she mock glared.

"Daddy almost said *shit*," Thomas announced.

"Tommy! You said a cuss!" James's eyes were wide as saucers.

"I did not."

"Yep, you sure did. That's fifty cents off your allowance." TJ gave Thomas his best dad look.

"Daddy! That's no fair!"

"I didn't say it, did I?"

Thomas slammed back against the booth, a full-on pout on his face.

"Hey." Monica put a hand on Thomas's arm. "This isn't the way to start the day, huh? Your choice, but I think you want to have a great day with your daddy."

"I do. I want to have a good day with you, Daddy. I didn't mean to be bad." His boy had his daddy's temperament, that was for sure.

TJ was constantly amazed at how Monica could turn a kid around. "I know, buddy. How about we wash the truck this afternoon when it's warmer? You can earn back that allowance."

"Oh, yes! I like to wash the truck!"

"Me too, Daddy? Me too? I'm big now." James looked more like him, all blue eyes and dark blond hair that would turn brown as he got older.

"Yessir. All of us."

"Yay!"

Lord have mercy, sometimes it ached how much he loved them. He shook his head, and Monica winked at him. Yeah, she knew.

The bell above the door jangled, and he glanced up again, wondering who else was coming to bitch at him today.

His teeth damn near fell out of his mouth as the Amazonian redhead, Macey Bene, waltzed in, pushing her brother Wacey in a wheelchair. "Hey, Jenny. My brother is craving huevos rancheros. Hook him up?"

"Hell, yes. Wacey Bene, what the hell happened to you?" Jenny went to clear off the one table that had a handicapped spot.

"My bones got nothin' on a horse's hooves."

Jenny scowled. "That ain't like you at all, honey."

"I know, right? I think there was a backfire right outside the holding pens. The lead mare went up, I went down, and the rest was history."

"Ouch."

"TJ, you're staring," Monica said, low enough only he and the boys could hear.

"Shit. Sorry." He sighed when the curse word popped out, because the kids would expect him to give Monica fifty cents. TJ tugged out his wallet and handed her a one. "Just in case."

"You'll probably need it, assuming the voice I hear is the voice I remember."

"Stop it."

The boys were both staring at him, and he didn't want to go into how he had an ex-boyfriend with his ex-wife sitting there. He and Monica were way more friendly than him and Wacey.

"Come on here to the back, Wacey. There'll be room for your chair. Chief! Look who's home!"

TJ looked up and met those deep brown eyes he remembered so well. "Wacey."

"Chief."

He could hear Macey mutter, "Oh, shit."

"Daddy! The lady said a cuss!" Little James couldn't keep his mouth shut for love or money.

"She did, but that's her business," Monica murmured.

"Sorry to hear you got hurt," TJ said, his cheeks burning.

"It happens to cowboys." Wacey's voice was dry as dust. "These your boys?"

"Yeah. Thomas and James. You remember Monica." This was frickin' weird.

"Yes, ma'am. Pleased. Sister, I'm sorry, but I ain't feeling like breakfast no more. Let's go on home."

"But, Bubba…."

"Macey." The single word was snapped like a broken tendon.

"You gonna turn tail and run like you always do, Bene?" TJ barked out the words, then had the urge to slap his hand over his mouth. He had to brazen it out now.

The entire restaurant had been staring at Wacey anyway, and now all eyes were on him. Fuck a duck sideways.

"You calling me a coward, you piece of shit? Because I will meet you outside and kick your ass even if you're packing heat and I'm in a wheelchair. You're still not a quarter of the man I am."

His sons stared back and forth from Wacey to TJ. He didn't want Thomas and James to see him lose his shit, but then again, he wasn't about to back down.

"Back off, Wacey. I misspoke." That was as close to an apology as he was going to get.

"You sure as shit did." Wacey didn't look away one second. Lord, that rage would be hot if it wasn't focused on him.

"Sorry, Jenny. I changed my mind," Macey said. "The air in here is sour." She began to pull Wacey away. "Sorry, Bubba. I forgot it was Friday. He's always in here later on Fridays."

"Well, I won't be back on Friday, then."

Jenny fluttered behind the counter. "Y'all go on and sit in the truck. I'll bring you an order out on the house."

"You don't have to…."

"Nonsense. Y'all are always welcome in here, Wacey. We're glad you're home."

"Thanks." Wacey set his jaw and stared over TJ's head until Macey wheeled him around to take him out.

"I'll pay for their breakfast," TJ said, feeling sheepish now that Wacey was out of sight. "I was out of line."

"I'll put it on your tab."

The boys were staring at him, James looking a little like he was fixin' to cry. "Daddy?"

"Hey, guys. I'm sorry. That's someone I used to know, and it made me mad to see him because we fought the last time we were together. Sometimes that happens. It's not very nice, and I apologize."

Monica watched him closely, and he knew she was trying to decide whether or not to say anything.

He shook his head slightly. They could talk about it when she came to get the boys.

"Okay, Daddy. Are we going to cook hamburgers on the grill for dinner tonight?"

"Is that what you both want?" He glanced at James, who still looked subdued.

"Uh-huh. I want." James defaulted to whatever his big brother said.

"Good deal. Maybe I'll make a few hot dogs too, huh? With cheese in the middle?"

"Oh, Daddy. Daddy, I love hot dogs!" That brought all the sunshine out in his baby boy.

"Do you?" He put on his best shocked face. Thank God neither of his babies were ones to dwell on things.

"Uh-huh. Better than… than…. Momma?"

"Better than chocolate cookies?" she offered.

"Oh. I like chocolate cookies…."

TJ grinned. "Better than broccoli."

"I don't like broccolis, Daddy. They give you the stinky poots."

"Ew!" Thomas wrinkled his nose. "Stanky butt."

Monica looked over at him. "They are your sons, Teej."

"They're boys. Of course, their momma can pass gas like a pit bull."

Both boys squealed like tires, and then they started bouncing.

"And on that note, I'm out of here. I'll have my phone if you need me. Love y'all." Monica kissed the boys, then smiled at TJ. "I'll pick them up Tuesday after school, yes?"

"Yes, ma'am."

Lord have mercy, he'd never doubted his girl would make it through nursing school, but working and getting her PA license might kill her.

TJ was on call all the damn time, but he tried to watch the boys as much as she needed him to. He adored all of them. Monica just hadn't been willing to settle for anything less than all of him.

"I'll see you hooligans later. Be good, you hear?"

"Yes, Momma!" The boys both saluted, which cracked TJ right up.

"Have a good weekend, Monica!" Jenny called. "Don't work too hard!"

"Never."

The boys looked at him expectantly. "More cancakes?"

"I think you've had enough, guys."

"Are we going home to your house?" James asked.

"We are. Who wants to go riding?" Both his sons were proficient on horseback, and their ponies needed exercising.

"Daddy!"

"Me! Me!"

"I want to ride Strawlberries!"

"It's Straw-Berry, James."

"Uh-huh. Strawlberries."

He didn't roll his eyes a bit. "Riding it is. Come on, you hooligans. Let's go have some fun."

Hopefully Wacey the Asshole Bene would be gone by the time they headed out.

Chapter Four

"SERIOUSLY, Sister? What the hell were you thinking?"

"That you wanted huevos. I forgot—"

"What?" Wacey snarled, just seeing red. "That me and Deputy Dawg fucked like bunnies?"

"Don't be nasty."

"Why not? Mr. Shithead Chief didn't feel constrained to be polite." Wacey shook his head. Babies. The man had two babies. He wanted to pretend he didn't know why that hurt so much, but he couldn't. He'd always fantasized that one day he'd come home and TJ would be waiting for him. "Why didn't y'all warn me?"

"I thought it would just hurt your feelings. So did Lace. I'm sorry, Dub."

"Me too. God, I'm sorry. I shouldn't have come home."

"Oh, for fuck's sake!" she snapped. "Stop being a pussy. Quit running away, you little shit. This is your home."

His eyes widened with a sudden, sharp fury. "I'm not a coward, you know. I don't fit in here."

"Well, no, it's not Austin. But God knows, if you need to get your gay go-go dancer on, you go to Santa Fe. They don't call it Santa Gay for nothing."

"Shut up!"

"What? You don't have stretch denim in your suitcase? Bondage straps?"

"Sister! You're pushing it."

"I have to get it out of my system," she said archly. "You know how hard it is to hold my snark with Mama and Pop?"

"Not to mention the thirty-seven-hundred kids you have. Be honest, are you trying to populate New Mexico?"

"No, I just seem to catch pregnant every time Tim walks through the room with a hard-on."

"Too much information, Sis. I mean, I thought you were trying to earn us another electoral vote."

"Oh, listen to you, smart boy." She pinched his arm, then jumped a mile and shrieked when someone knocked on the truck window.

"Your food," the kid said when Macey rolled down the window. "Jenny says thanks for waiting."

"Tell her thank you for the food." She took it and handed it over. "Spoiled brat."

"Fuck you." He didn't feel so spoiled. He hurt—his body, his heart, his soul. He ached, bone-deep.

More than anything, he just wanted to go back to doing his job, to pretend none of this had ever happened. He couldn't, and Wacey knew it. His leg was messed-up but good, and he had a lot of physical therapy to do once he healed. He was going to do it, though, and head back on the road as soon as he could.

The damn horses had lost their minds like a hornet's nest had been tossed in with them. It just didn't make sense. He hadn't felt even a second of worry before that lead mare had reared.

Wacey knew horses. Knew their signals. That was why he'd told Pop it had to be a noise or something. A bee sting. Anything but her temperament.

Once his broken shoulder healed, he'd be able to use the crutches, start really working, and go the fuck back to Austin. It shouldn't take long before he could take the weight of running the rodeo off his little brother's shoulders. Kace was a kickass stock manager, but he knew Kace wouldn't be into managing the whole thing for long. Kace was just a baby.

"You're thinking loud enough to wake the dead. You want to take the food home? I know it's tough with your shoulder." Macey actually could do sympathetic when she wanted to. Not that she wanted to very often, from what he could see, but that was her business, he reckoned.

"Yeah. Please." He wasn't hungry anyway. He'd just wanted to get the fuck out of the house, away from all the eyes watching him. He wasn't used to that anymore.

Everyone in Turquoise knew everyone's business. They all had a nose in their neighbor's garden. That was the great thing about a place like Austin. You could know folks but not be all up in their daily business. You could have friends without the constant baggage.

"No problem." She got them moving, heading back toward the ranch.

They passed the weird little art galleries and the chichi restaurants that were only open from eleven to three Friday through Sunday, the antique stores, and the strip mall with nothing but fabric and yarn and pottery studios. It was all very touristy, at least on the weekends when they had walks and strolls and festivals and fiestas. The crowds were already starting to trickle in from the Duke City and Santa Fe.

The river really lit up this time of year.

The little groups of adobe houses started then, pockets of hippies and New Agers, artists and pagans, little gardens and gorgeous roses before the fruit and vegetable stalls and the horse farms started. It hadn't changed a bit.

They finally made it to the ranch, to the huge wooden sign that said, "Bene Ranch and Rodeo School," and Macey got his chair out of the back of the truck after she parked in front of the main house. "Come on, Bro. Let's get you in and heat this shit up so we can eat."

"Thanks, Sister. Seriously. What are we going to tell Mama?"

"The truth. That I got to the diner and decided I wanted to come home and you didn't mind."

"Thank you."

"Anytime, Bubba." She gave him a grin that spoke of their childhood together, of all the trouble they'd gotten into.

He settled in the chair with her help. Wacey was not used to feeling helpless. He hated it.

"It won't last long. The therapist said crutches in three weeks, right?"

"Yeah. And I have a lot of balloons to blow up before that."

"You do! I can't wait to post pictures of that on Instagram."

"I will kick your ass."

"You and what healthy army?" Macey shot back.

"The bullfighters like me best."

"Yeah, maybe the ones on the road."

He winced, but nodded. Yeah, no shit. The guys at the school were all retired, mostly because of his decisions, and they didn't adore him.

Macey wheeled him inside, then heated up breakfast, and made him a plate of his eggs.

He had to admit they were good—spicy and rich, just like he liked them. Jenny's cooks did an amazing job. Even with the tortillas steamed a little from reheating, they were delish.

Mama popped her head into the kitchen, frowning. "I thought you wanted to go out."

"I decided I wanted to come home, Mama. It was so crowded in there." Macey went to Mama and hugged her. "It's better at home."

"Well, I would have made you bring me hash browns."

"Jenny sent extra for you. Want me to heat them up?"

"I've got some bacon grease from Pop's breakfast this morning. I'll use that."

"Is there still some bacon left, Mama?" he asked. Bacon was just what this needed.

"Of course, mijo."

"You rock." He felt better already. Maybe he'd just needed some food. And to not see TJ. Jesus, what a fucker.

Kids. Two kids and a wife. Fuck.

He wanted his fantasy back.

Not that the man had ever lied to him.

"I want a normal life, man. I'm not going to ride the rodeo and be the token queer cowboy. I want a house and a family. I want something real."

Those words let Wacey know that it was over. Real. TJ had wanted something real. Obviously he was a fucking figment of TJ's imagination.

He'd left that night and hadn't ever come back. His people had come to him, in twos and threes and tens, but he'd never been able to come back and see what TJ had thought real was.

Now he knew. It was two boys and a girl from the high school class below theirs.

"What is it, mijo?" His mama saw all.

"Nothing. I just need to take some Advil." Wacey had already given up the pain pills the doc had prescribed. They made him queasy as hell, made him goofy too.

"I'll get them," Macey said, as Lacey and Pop walked in.

Hail, hail, the gang's all here.

There was a flurry of heating and cooking, and he had another plate of migas, these homemade, and some bacon. In no time.

Who needed the café and TJ holding court like some feudal lord?

Not him. No sir. This was their place, and they loved him here.

Even if they drove him out of his friggin' cabeza.

Chapter Five

TJ watched the kids wash the truck. Well, trucks. Josh had come over to borrow his leaf blower, and he'd stuck around to get James and Thomas to wash his truck too.

They sat in lawn chairs, Josh with a beer, TJ with a Coke. He tried not to drink when the kids were around, just because they kept him on his toes and he needed to be sharp.

Josh burped, then gave him a sideways look. "I hear you and Wacey Bene had words. Couldn't even wait until he'd been home a week?"

"Shut up."

"Seriously. In the café? In front of the boys and Monica?" Josh was just needling him now.

"Are you deaf? I said hush." He grinned wryly. "My mouth ran away with my brain. It just popped out."

"It's always been that way with y'all, I swear. I thought you two were going to combust back in the day."

His cheeks heated. "I did too." TJ sighed. "He looks like hell. That shocked me, you know? I still—well. You missed a spot, James!"

"Sorry, Daddy!" The hose sprayed again.

"Does he? I heard those horses damn near killed him. He was in the hospital for a couple weeks."

"I wonder what happened. Wacey is never careless with horses. Ever. It's like he has a sixth sense with what they'll do."

"I got nothing. I mean, maybe he just screwed up. It happens."

"I guess." None of them were getting any younger, right? "I'm sorry the kids were there. Maybe I ought to stop by his folks' place and apologize."

"Ooh. The law crossing the borders of the lawless West…."

Yeah. The Benes were sort of a royal family around here, and no one dared to trespass on the rodeo company's land, lest they get their asses handed to them. Between the family, the dogs, and the cowboys either bunking, training, or teaching there? It was intense.

Still, if he went in his squad car….

"Just stay away," Josh told him. "Healthier for all of you."

"Yeah, you're probably right." Still, Wacey Bene was the finest man he'd ever known, even torn straight to hell. Just thinking about all those days and nights they'd spent together made him sweat.

God knew, he loved Monica, and they'd had a good relationship, but Wacey had always been TJ's one true thing. The one true thing that he'd screwed up royally.

Christ.

"Stop. Live in the moment, buddy. Your oldest son is peeing on your agave."

"Thomas!" Lord have mercy.

"What?" Thomas turned, spraying like a tomcat as he did.

"Ew!" James turned the hose on Thomas, and it was on.

Sadly, Thomas would lose flow before James did.

"Wow. Is it wrong to hope for a girl?"

"Oh buddy. Monica can pull some gross shit. There's no guarantee."

"Can she?" Josh looked so surprised. "My girl is kinda dainty."

"She's still in the honeymoon period, no matter how long you've been together. Once you see her give birth, she'll give that up for Lent."

"I have to watch?"

"Buddy, I tell you, it's worth it." He wouldn't have missed a second of his boys coming into the world, wouldn't have asked that Monica face that alone. He'd never been more awed by her, and the fact was, she was the best woman he'd ever known, along with his momma.

Josh grinned. "Okay, I'll take your word for it and hang in there."

He winked, then looked at his totally drenched boys. "Y'all want to go soak in the hot tub?"

"Hot tub!" They all but fell over themselves in their rush to finish rinsing the trucks.

"You want to soak, buddy?"

"If my studly body doesn't get you all hot, yeah."

"You've never done a thing for me, Josh."

Josh made a face. "Wounded."

They started laughing, then hooting, and then it was all over but the crying.

TJ got up so he could turn off the hose, then take the cover off the hot tub. He locked it, and not just for the boys' safety. He had neighbors who would help themselves. TJ at least wanted them to ask, and to wear suits.

He treated the water and got it warming and pulled towels out of the little cabana he'd made.

TJ loved his place. He had about ten acres, just enough to run five or six horses and have room to move. His acreage was long and narrow, which let him have neighbors, but also a way to get away from them.

Josh brought out four bottles of water, and they settled in, the boys "swimming" in the bubbles.

"You got a good setup," Josh said, and not for the first time. "I was thinking of doing something like this, but I reckon it will have to wait now."

"I don't think you want to bubble in one of these if you're pregnant. After though, sure."

"Yeah. The doc says regular baths are okay, though."

TJ could just picture his usually laconic buddy asking the doctor a zillion questions. So cute.

"I can't wait to watch her body change, to know why."

He smiled and nodded. Monica had been different every day. The wonder he still felt at the fact that they'd made two little people never seemed far away.

"It's good, to have someone to talk to, huh?"

He got that. He'd spilled his heart out to Josh more times than he could say. Including today.

"Daddy, I'm a narwhal." Thomas made his arm into a horn on his nose.

Josh winked at him before asking, "What the heck is a narwhal?"

"A fish with a toothpick on his face."

"Oh. Really?"

"Uh-huh. I learned it in school."

"Neat. I like toothpicks." Josh was always about the simple parts. Not that he wasn't bright. Just… really good with the kids. He would make a great dad.

"The show Daddy watches with the mean mans? The one man chews a toothpick all the time. Daddy says that's nasty." James never missed anything, he swore.

"But they can be useful if you only use them when you're supposed to." Josh always made things sound so reasonable, even when he was talking crap.

"Yeah. They're kinda sharp." James floated over to him, still little enough to need cuddles from scary things like wooden toothpicks.

TJ gave them willingly. Someday they wouldn't need him at all. Wow. He was getting maudlin. He blamed Wacey Bene.

He fucking hated knowing he was to blame for the whole thing too. Not that he'd change having his boys or loving Monica, but Wacey had deserved to know that it wasn't him. TJ had been the one who hadn't been able to face his family and his town and admit he was gay.

Obviously Wacey had brazened it out. On tour at the rodeo, for fuck's sake. Wacey had always been the brave one, the one to say I love you first, the one to make TJ crazy with his teasing and then not teasing leading to wild sex. To ask for TJ to commit to them.

He accused Wacey of running, but TJ was the one who'd walked away. Scared to death.

"You cool, man?" Josh looked at him with knowing eyes, but Josh always knew. Always. Fucker.

"I am." He smiled down at James. And if he wasn't, well, if there was one thing TJ knew how to do, it was fake it until he could make it.

He was the king of that.

Chapter Six

WACEY sat on the front porch panting with exertion, the arm crutches feeling awkward and painful. Still, this was better than the chair.

He wasn't a chair kind of guy. He was a cowboy, dammit. He had all the respect in the world for guys like Jerome Davis, but he could walk, and he was going to manage it, by God.

It would be easier if walking from the front room to the porch wasn't so frigging hard.

Mama did like her shit, and it was everywhere, waiting to jump into his path.

Pop had taken Mama into Albuquerque to go to Vernon's, and the ladies were at the Ranch House shooting pool. He was it, because most of the hands were up to town.

He grabbed his phone to call Kace, see how things were doing.

"Whut?"

"Don't 'whut' me, you little shit. What's up? How's it doing?"

Kace was a kid, but smart as a whip and about as fierce as any cowboy he'd ever met. "Good. Real good. We just set off the fireworks for the closer, and I'm shipping all them out to the carnies. I got to tell you, Bubba, it's humid here."

"You in Fayetteville?" He hated the humidity. He forgot until he got here and breathed the desert air again.

"I am. How you feeling, man?"

"I'm on the crutches now. I'll be back at work soon, I hope."

"Good. Good. You don't worry, though. I got this."

He wasn't sure if he hoped so or if he'd be pissed because he didn't have a place anymore. Fuck. Fuck, of course he hoped so! Kacey was his little brother, and his sibs were his best friends, for fuck's sake. Of course he wanted Kace to have it under control, right?

Right.

"All right, man. You have a good night. Holler at me tomorrow?"

He heard Kacey laugh, and he wasn't sure if Kace was listening to him or someone else on the arena.

"Kace?"

"Right. Will do. Gotta go. Talk at you later."

"Bye."

Then he was left with dead air, him and the puppers. Who were barking their damned fool heads off at the main horse barn.

"What's up, y'all?" He frowned, moving toward the railing of the porch. "Someone in there?"

He heard one of the mares whinny, the sound high, almost panicked.

"I'm coming." He reached inside the front door, grabbed the rifle, and strapped it on, then headed out, dragging his happy ass down the stairs and across the dirt.

He was panting, hoping it was a varmint and not some kind of human thief or a teenager looking for trouble.

The horses were all out of the barn, tossing their heads and stomping, warning him that something was wrong and they weren't happy. He stared a moment, not wanting to startle them, but something about their agitation niggled at him.

Okay. Okay, he could brace his elbow on one crutch, then maybe set up the other to hold his forearm where he'd get the rifle extended. It took some work, but he got settled, eight feet from the barn entrance. "Whoever you are, I got a rifle trained on your ass. You come on out of there."

He swore to God that he was going to kill somebody if they were hurting his horses.

"What the fuck?" Dee came running up, the old roper limping as bad as he was. "What's wrong, Dub?"

"Someone's in the barn, Dee."

"I got your back." *Oh good. A broke-dick cowboy and a rope with two and a half fingers in total. Faboo.*

"I'll cover you." He was about to start laughing hysterically.

"You got your phone? Call your sisters if you do. I'll go look." Dee was a good man.

"I'm coming with you. Together, we got this."

To Dee's credit, he didn't laugh. Instead, he spat on the ground, then nodded. "All right, son. I'd put you up against a passel of wildcats, even all broke."

"Thanks." He handed off the rifle to Dee before heading into the barn. He wanted to make sure no one was in there doing something to his animals.

The smell of gas was wrong. No one brought gasoline in the barn. Never. It was stored in a metal building half a pasture away.

Dee stopped dead. "Stay back, son. If someone is waiting to light this bitch, we'd both be dead."

"I didn't survive a trampling to get burnt up, sir."

"No, I reckon you didn't." Dee stuck his head around the door of the barn. "Gloomy in there. I don't see anyone, but we need to check the stalls. They're all empty, but I didn't see Dozer the donkey in the yard."

"I'll take the left. Holler if you find the gas." He started opening stall doors, one after another, hunting for animals or gasoline.

He found Dozer in the last stall, and he would bet their would-be arsonist hadn't even seen him. He was sleeping standing up, and the little guy was half-deaf with age. "Hey, buddy. Let's get you out of here, huh? We'll put you in the foaling barn until we figure out the gas smell."

Dozer's ears picked up, and the donkey nuzzled him, following him easily, swaying side to side.

Wacey patted Dozer's neck. "I know, buddy. You were what? Three when I left? But you remember me. I love that."

"You smell like family, I bet," Dee said. "The last stall had three gas cans. I've pulled them out."

He glanced at Dee, worried. "Should we call the cops?"

"My vote is we wait for the boss, but it's your call."

"Shit. We'll manage it. Let's spray out that stall, just in case. I'll text Lace and them."

"You got it." Dee limped off, while he slowly led poor Dozer out to mingle with the horses. He wouldn't wander off with them there, and the paddock was fenced.

He balanced again so he could pull out his phone and text his sisters.

Problem at the barn. Need you two

On the way

He knew the girls and Derek and Tim would be headed his direction—there was nothing like problems to get his sisters moving. They could be seriously motivated at the smell of trouble when an emotional plea could make them scoff.

Cowgirls were tough.

Thank God Macey's brood was at their paternal granny's, and the twins were at someone's house spending the night.

By the time they had the stall cleaned out, the girls were home, Derek helping Wacey's screaming body back up to the house while Tim finished spraying the stall and the girls cross-examined Dee.

"Just put me on the porch, and I'll keep an eye out for you." He didn't want to leave any of his family in harm's way.

"Will do. Shit, you've got to be dying, man. I been where you are."

"I know. Go on. Make sure none of those horses kick Lace."

Derek nodded and pelted off to help. Some of those horses had been laid up in the barn due to injury, so the sisters would be worried about them.

He sat there, starting to shake, good and hard. Not trembling, full-body shaking, feet thrumming on the porch.

"Shit, son." Dee was there somehow, two of the border collies at his sides. "Come on and get inside. If there was anyone out there, they've gone."

Dee looked frail, but there wasn't a weak bone in that man's body. He disappeared into the house, then returned to muscle Wacey into his wheelchair. "You got some shock. You need to get your feet up and get under a blanket."

"Don't tell none of them."

"No. No, I wouldn't."

"Thank you." He panted, his whole body feeling like he had the flu, aching and chilled. God, he hated this. He was ready to be whole again. To do his damned job.

Dee wrapped a blanket around him, got him a bottle of water, and settled him with his feet up. The fact that Dee didn't put him to bed like a child made him glad. The couch was good enough while he waited for the report from the family.

Too bad he missed it when one of the dogs curled up with him to warm him and he fell clean asleep.

Chapter Seven

"CHIEF! Can I speak to you?"

Shit. TJ paused on the steps of the post office, the mail for the office in his hand. The staff admin was very, very pregnant. Seemed to be something in the water. So when Maria'd seen him sitting at his desk playing Criminal Case on his iPad, she'd put him to work getting the mail.

"Sure, Miz Ruth. What can I do for you?"

"I was at the Friends of the Library meeting with Flora Bene, and she was telling us that someone tried to burn down their barns Friday night! Her boy, the one that's on crutches? He went down there and ended up back in the hospital Friday night."

"Oh, hell." He hadn't heard that, but they would have to take him to the Burque anyway. Turquoise was too small for a hospital. "Is he home now?"

"Yes, but… is there an arsonist? You'd say if we needed to watch, wouldn't you?"

"Of course I would." He tapped the envelopes he held in one hand against the opposite palm. "I'll look into it, Miz Ruth. I have no doubt it was just some kids, or the Benes would have called us."

"Oh good. Poor Flora was just gray and tired."

"That's not right. She's such a bright force of nature." He needed to see who was on duty, who he could send out.

"Exactly. I knew you would want to handle this yourself."

He was going to bite something. Maybe her. "Yes, ma'am. Good evening."

"Have a good one, Chief." She waved at him.

He did not stomp. Law enforcement officers did not stomp off when a citizen asked them to do a welfare check.

That didn't mean he didn't want to pout and growl and go home and have a beer instead of driving all the way out to the Bene Ranch to see a bunch of people who didn't want to see him.

He did it, though, mainly because whatever happened put Wacey Bene back in the hospital, and that was bullshit. He'd been keeping track, and he knew Wacey had gone from wheelchair to arm crutches. So, yeah. Not cool.

TJ detoured to drop off his mail before grabbing his jacket. "I'm off to the Bene Ranch, Maria. I'll have my radio on."

"Give them all my love, Chief. Lace and Macey sure ran out of the Ranch House like their asses were on fire Friday night."

"Did they? Where the hell was I?"

"Sleeping. Friday morning there was that big collision with that tourist bus."

"Right. That makes me feel better."

"They didn't call it in, Chief."

"No, I did look at the reports for the weekend." He grinned at her. "Thanks, hon." He left the office, humming under his breath. It was a pretty drive, at least.

The giant wooden sign that marked the Bene Ranch was like a huge "Keep Out," and he noticed that, in all the years he'd worked for the police department, no one had been called out. All those cowboys and not one theft, not one fight?

They were like law unto themselves. Not just ranch people, but rodeo people.

He pulled up by the ranch house, and a pack of dogs went nuts, barking and wagging. The wagging made him decide they weren't going to eat him, so he got out of the car, murmuring low.

Harrison "Pop" Bene came out to the car, whistling once and waving the dogs off. "Chief Cook. What can I do you for?"

"Afternoon, Pop. I was just doing a courtesy check. I hear you had some vandalism in your barn Friday night."

"Someone let the horses out and put gasoline cans in the barn. Dub heard them and headed out, but he didn't see anyone."

"So no one was actually out there, but they left gas cans?" Now that was an odd thing. Why would someone go to all that trouble if they weren't going to light that fire? "You think I could speak to Wacey?"

"Sure. He's in the kitchen. I've got an appointment at the bank, or I'd show you in. You remember the way?"

"Yessir. Thank you." He ducked into the house, hoping like hell he didn't run into Lacey or Macey. They would kick his ass right out.

Who he found was Wacey and Flora, both drinking coffee. Wacey was in a big, overstuffed chair there at the kitchen table. That was a cool idea, wasn't it?

He nodded to them both, putting on his business face. "Afternoon, Miz Flora. Wacey, can I speak to you about Friday night? Pop said you were the one home."

"I was. I didn't see who was there, though. It was damn near dark. I heard the horses."

"Did Pop call you?" Flora asked.

"No, ma'am. You know how it is in town. But a few people have expressed concern that we might have an arsonist, so I wanted to check into it."

Wacey looked like hammered shit, pale as milk and too damn skinny for his own good. "Whoever it was, they didn't know to look for the donkey."

TJ blinked. "Dozer? Shit, is he still alive? Pardon my French."

"He is. He's a little mangy and half-deaf, but totally alive."

"Wow."

"Sit down, TJ." Flora rose to pour him a cup of coffee. "Cream and one sugar?"

"Yes, ma'am." Holy crap. She remembered? Really?

She served him a cup. "I'll be right back. Wacey, you don't wear yourself out."

Wacey nodded, and then they were alone.

"You think she went to yell at your dad?" TJ asked.

"Pop's heading to the bank. She's just not sure what to do with the two of us in the same room."

"Oh." TJ sat. "Heard you were in the hospital. You gonna live?" How fucking weird was this? Look at them, all carefully civilized.

"I just pushed too hard is all. I'll be riding in a few days, then I'll be able to tag Kace and let him have a day off."

A few months, maybe. TJ didn't say it, though. He was a professional, damn it.

"So, no one there. Horses out, donkey in. Three gas cans. Did you keep them?"

"Yeah, but Dee was all over them. He carried them out to the shed."

"Dee wouldn't have a reason to do this, would he?" He knew better, but he had to ask hard questions.

Wacey snorted. "Shit. Our Dee? He'd cut his own arm off before he hurt us."

"I thought so. No tire tracks, no vehicles that you heard?" Why would someone random come in from outside to fuck with the Benes? Hell, why would they do it, knowing Wacey was sitting there at home?

"Not that I saw, man, but I was sort of convulsing by the time they brought me in."

"Shit. Okay. You mind if I talk to Dee?"

"Let me text him. He's down at the roping pens, I reckon."

"Thanks." He sat there, knowing he shouldn't stare. He did it anyway. Wacey could have been his whole life, if he'd let it happen.

He hadn't.

Wacey grabbed his phone and texted, fingers flying like magic. Damn. It took a minute, then a soft yodeling sounded. "He says it'll be a few minutes, but he'll be here."

"Thanks." TJ had no idea what else to say, even if there were a zillion questions battering at the back of his throat trying to get out. *What happened that you got hurt? Are you broke bad? What the hell am I doing here at the Bene Ranch when the law didn't come out here?*

The Benes policed themselves, and yet he was sitting here at the kitchen table.

Wacey didn't chatter either, though. He sat there, watching TJ with a quiet, calculating expression.

TJ fought the urge to squirm. Finally he had to say something. "What? You're staring at me."

"I haven't seen you in a long time. You've gotten old."

"Fuck you. You look like shit off a dog's ass."

"That surprises no one. I just got out of a coma."

"You always know what to say to make me feel like a jerk." TJ sighed, taking off his hat to rub his head, which ached fiercely.

"If the shoe fits, Chief." This time Wacey winked, so he couldn't even snarl.

"What happened, Wacey? You never miss a beat with the horses."

"It was an accident. There was a sound like a backfire, right there in the paddock, and the lead mare lost her shit, taking the rest with her."

"Like a backfire, or a backfire?" Something pushed at his brain, amorphous but kinda slimy.

"Like. There weren't any cars close."

"Huh." It seemed unlikely, what he was thinking, so he kept it to himself. "How are you otherwise?"

"Tired. Ready to go home and get back to work, but it'll be a bit. Probably the next season."

"Go home? You got a place in Texas now?" Surely Wacey would have gone there if someone was waiting on him.

"I rent a condo in Austin, yeah."

Now he couldn't imagine that at all. Mr. Lives and Breathes Horses renting a condo? TJ blinked. "You got a chichi boyfriend?"

"Pardon me? Why would I be here if I had someone that could—"

"Sorry, Dub. I was back at the roping pens. Chief? You needed me?"

Damn it. Wacey had been getting all riled up and was about to spill information.

TJ smiled at the old cowboy he'd known his whole life. "Hey, Dee. You were there Friday night, right? With the gas cans?"

"Yessiree-bob. You shoulda seen Dub. He was packing and fixin' to shoot whoever was screwing with the horses, crutches or no."

"That sounds familiar. You did some digging after. No tire tracks? No ATVs? No way to know how someone got here?"

"I'd guess four-wheelers. No way it was horses."

"There's so many tire tracks out there all the time, though." Wacey shrugged. "Lacey and Derek looked the next morning, but there was nothing obvious."

"Okay. Dee, Wacey said you found the gas cans. Can you tell me what it looked like in the stall?"

"Stacked real neat, like they was intending to come back or something. I mean, if I was gonna do it, I'd light and toss, spread the gas everywhere."

"But Dee, the smell was everywhere."

"I know, Dub. That was the weird part. It was like them cans had been down there awhile and someone came later to let them horses out."

That piqued his interest even more. "But the gas hadn't been spread into the straw or the aisle?"

"Nope. They was just sitting there."

"Okay. Anyone you can think that would have a grudge that wouldn't know about the donkey?"

"Dub?"

Wacey shrugged. “Y’all’d know better than me.”

“Not that I know of,” Dee said. “I’ll ask around, though.”

“Okay.” TJ stood. “Thanks for your time, guys. If anything else happens that’s odd, please call me. I know you folks take care of your own, but if this is something that might start to spread, I’ll need to know.”

“Maybe it was kids stealing gas? Did you check the work trucks, Dee?” Wacey asked.

“Carlos did it.” Dee sighed. “He said nothing was out of place. No one had siphoned from the private tank, according to the level.”

“Dammit. I thought I was being all clever and shit.”

TJ chuckled. “Trust me, in law enforcement, most of the crap we think of is more clever than the actual criminal.”

“Yeah?” Wacey shrugged with one shoulder. “That would be my favorite part.”

“Coming up with crazy stuff? I do it a lot. Well, and I play Criminal Case on Facebook.”

Wacey’s cheeks went bright red, and he knew he’d found another addict.

How weird would it be to friend his ex on Facebook? He knew Jenny at the diner had all three of her exes on her account.

“Y’all kids and your electronics.” Dee cackled, the sound merry as hell.

“You should see Kace. He’s attached to his phone by his dick.”

“We’re crazy, right? Also, TMI, Wacey. Seriously.” He winked at Wacey, who actually laughed. “Walk me out, Dee?”

“Surely do. You good, Dub?”

“Totally fine. I’ll stay right here.”

"Take care of yourself, Wacey." He figured he should say it.

"I do. Always. Tell Monica and the boys I apologize for having to go before."

"I will. I get the boys again on Saturday." TJ lifted one hand in a wave before heading out with Dee. They stopped on the porch. "I'm serious, Dee. Call me if anything else happens? This is too weird to be an isolated incident, I think."

"Will do. You know he's hurt bad, right? Tore up."

"I know. He was in the hospital until what? Sunday?"

"Yeah. Pop Bene said his system was just overwhelmed."

"That sucks. You keep an eye out for any more signs of a firebug. I'll either stop by or have one of my guys drive through in a few days."

He just wanted to make sure no one burned down the rodeo school. That would put a real crimp in their economy.

Maybe he'd get to see Wacey again on top of all that.

Maybe he'd friend the little fuck on Facebook.

Chapter Eight

"DUB, you sure you're okay on your own?"

"Pop, I've run things for ten years. I can spend a Wednesday night on my own."

The kids had some soccer thing, and everyone was going. Everyone but him. He was out of the chair again, but it had been therapy day, and he was wore to the bone.

"Well, last time we left you alone didn't go so well." Pop winked, but Wacey knew worry lurked under that easy grin.

"I know. I promise to be good, Pop. I swear."

"I know, son." Pop sighed. "You call us if you need us." Pop patted his good shoulder.

"Will do." He waited until they were gone, and then he stood to grab him a cup of coffee. It was better than a beer, which was what he really wanted.

This sucked. As in giant hairy donkey balls. At least the sisters had made Pop put in good Wi-Fi. He should play Criminal Case. Maybe look in on TJ's Facebook now he knew TJ had one.

He opened his tablet and started goofing off, chattering at folks on the circuit, playing games, listening to music.

A scream from the stables had him up and moving, his phone in hand.

As soon as 911 answered, he barked, "I need someone at the Bene Ranch. Now."

His crutches got all tangled up at the stairs, and he almost went down, but Wacey staggered back upright, moving as fast as his body would let him.

The 911 dispatcher was talking to him, but he didn't have the coordination or the breath to chat. He just hung up and kept moving toward the barn.

I'm coming, guys. I'll help.

He wasn't sure who was in there, but Maisey and Buttercup were having a cat, the sounds furious. Then Dozer started up, the hee-haw, hee-haw hysterical, and the fucking dogs were losing their collective shits.

"I swear to God if you hurt my donkey, I will kill you!" Wacey shouted.

He never saw the blow to the back of the head. All he saw was lights and then darkness.

Well fuck a doodle goddamn doo.

TJ drove like his ass was on fire. He'd been on the way back to his house when he heard the all-unit call for someone to go to the Bene Ranch. So he radioed and took the assignment, flipping on his lights and sirens.

Shit. Shit, what the hell was going on now?

He pulled up to the house—which was lit up, the french doors wide open. The horses were milling about, Dozer the donkey braying like the world was coming to an end.

"Fuck." He went into cop mode, ducking out of his car and drawing his sidearm. Okay, house first. He would secure it, then start with the barn nearest the house, where the gas can incident had happened. He should call for backup, but he had all of two officers—Jack was in Albuquerque with his wife having supper, and Mike, who was on a call in Madrid or something, for heaven's sake.

He took the porch steps two at a time, seeing an iPad, a single cup of coffee. Okay, one person. "Wacey? Anyone in here?"

The donkey brayed again, and he glanced out, seeing someone moving out there on the ground.

Shit. He leaped back down the stairs and ran flat-out to the prone form, the dogs all running out to bark at him, protecting whoever had fallen.

"Good boys. Good pups. Wacey?" Sure as shit, Wacey was trying to sit up, the knot on the back of his head looking like a goose egg. "Wacey, what happened?"

"I don't know."

"Stay there." He had to clear the barn, and then he would come back for Wacey. "Stay, pups."

About three-quarters of the pack listened, but the others followed him, curious and wagging.

He slowed at the barn door, easing around the frame to check his danger areas. His heart pounded, because God knew he was better at going to meetings these days than he was at active duty.

"Police," he announced. "Show yourself!"

No one answered, and he didn't get shot, so that was both good and bad. Bad because he wanted to figure out who was doing this. Good because he could go back to Wacey and determine if he needed medical.

He checked the stalls real quick, but there was nothing there. Just open doors.

Okay. Back to the downed victim. He turned on his boot heel and headed out to meet Wacey, who was on his hands and knees, retching. Oh, man.

"Hey. Hey, take it easy. I'll call an ambulance."

"No. No. You can't. They'll never leave me ever again."

"But you've got to have a concussion, Wace." He put a hand on Wacey's back. "Where were you when they hit you?"

"Heading for the barns. My phone? You see it?"

He traced his steps and found the phone maybe three feet from the barn door, off to the left. The dispatcher had disconnected, but the history showed 911.

"Why is it…? God, help me in?"

"I got you. Grab your crutches." He waited for Wacey to kinda… climb him, getting his crutches in hand. Then TJ just picked Wacey clean up off the ground.

Jesus, the man didn't weigh as much as a bird. He'd forgotten. Maybe Wacey was even skinnier now.

Or maybe TJ was full-size now and stronger than he'd been then.

He hauled Wacey into the house, heading for the couch in the front room. "At least let me call someone to come look. Monica might be off duty. She's a nurse."

"No. No, I'll be fine. Really. I can see. You can hang with me for a second, but don't tell anyone, man."

"Okay." Damn it, he didn't like any of this. TJ moved to the kitchen to grab a towel and wet it so he could wash off the blood and look at Wacey's wound.

It was a goose egg, sure as shit, but it was already starting to settle. Lord, that was gonna be a bruise. "Where are your people, Wace?"

"Soccer game."

"Who all knew they were leaving you here alone?" There was no possible arson here. This was a flat-out attack on Wacey.

"I don't know. No one. Everyone. I mean, I told my PT guy in Albuquerque I didn't think I was going to make it to the kids' games."

"Man, that makes my job harder." TJ grinned. "Here, hold this on your head. You want a cold drink?"

"Please. Not a beer."

"Yeah, no." That would be a terribly bad idea. He found Sprite instead, poured some over ice in a lidded cup. One of those things with a straw. He took it back into the front room, finding Wacey lying back on the couch, the towel under his head, a border collie licking his hand. "You still alive?"

"I am. Risha here isn't sure, though. She's considering eating me."

"I think she's trying to resuscitate. Here." He handed Wacey the drink, then helped him ease up to half sitting so he could have some. "Okay, start at the top."

"I was playing on Facebook, and I heard the horses. I called 911, but I couldn't talk and walk. I headed to the barns, and… that's it. There's nothing else."

"Nothing at all? What kinds of noises did you hear? What were the horses doing?"

"Screaming. I heard a scream. A person scream."

"A person. Are you sure? Barn cats get caught under hooves…."

"I heard a scream. Short. Sharp. A real scream. Do you think it was a mountain lion got in the barn?"

"I don't know, but no mountain lion is going to hit you over the head. As soon as you're sure you're okay, I'll go do some more searching."

"Right." Wacey snorted, then winked at him. "I forgot about that part."

"Well, you did get hit on the head." He chuckled.

"I don't know what you're talking about."

"You sure you don't want me to see if Monica is available?"

"You don't know if your wife's at work, man?"

"Huh?" TJ blinked. "Monica? Well, since she's my ex, I try not to ask her for a written schedule every week."

Wacey's eyes went wide, and maybe if he hadn't just been whacked on the head, he wouldn't have looked gobsmacked.

That gave TJ a little bit of a happy. "Yep, I'm single again and lookin' for love in all the wrong places. You need anything else before I head back to the barn?"

"Nah. I'm okay. I'm going to sit."

"Keep the dog with you, and yell your bumped head off if you need me." He had to get out there before too much more time passed. There was no real forensics team in their tiny county, and the state police wouldn't come out for something this amorphous and, in their opinion, minor.

He just couldn't figure out who the fuck would want to hurt Wace. Here. Now.

The light was really fading, so he got a flashlight out of his car, knowing it would help get everything together, let him see smaller details.

He wasn't even sure what the fuck he was looking for.

In the end, he found a few footprints that weren't his or Wacey's, but they were mostly obscured by the horse tracks. He checked the donkey's stall, since he'd obviously been let out this time.

Nothing. Dammit.

He hit the back entrance to the barn, but again, there was nada, so TJ headed back to the house to check in on Wacey. This was obviously a series of crimes of opportunity. He wasn't gonna let someone have another shot tonight.

Wacey was standing at the kitchen sink, swaying just a little.

"Hey! Hey, what are you doing, man?" He caught Wacey just as he almost swayed too far.

"I'm a little queasy. I was going to grab some grapes."

"I'll get you some. Back to your couch." He felt so weird, touching Wacey Bene again after so long. Even skinny and injured, Wacey made his heart beat faster.

"Thank you. I vote that I don't get whacked again."

"I agree. In fact I would love for you to stop getting hurt altogether." He wrestled Wacey back to the couch, then went to get some grapes out of the…. They were in a drainer in a sink. Stubborn man.

He shook them out and got them in a bowl, then found himself sitting next to Wacey on the sofa, handing him a bowl of grapes.

"Thanks again. You probably have somewhere to be."

"You trying to get rid of me, bud?" he teased.

"No. I'm trying to keep from collapsing on you."

"I'll stay until someone comes home." He knew Wacey didn't want his family to know about this incident, but that wasn't realistic.

"If they find out, they'll never leave me alone, ever again."

"I know, but someone is trying to hurt you, Wacey."

"Someone's doing a pretty damn good job, Chief."

"They are. Think hard. I know your head hurts. Who would want to damage you, man?" He had the strongest urge to hold Wacey's hand. Probably wouldn't be welcome.

"I haven't been home in ten years. Half these guys wouldn't know me from Job."

"Huh. Maybe one of them thinks you're a threat now you're home? A manager or something?" TJ was grasping at straws, and he knew it.

"I can ask Lacey and Derek, but I don't think so. I'm in charge of the show out there, or I was."

"You will be again, I'm sure." Jesus, he was sappy if that idea hurt his feelings. "Eat your grapes, Wace."

"Yeah. Thanks." Wacey ate a few, then grinned at him, the look pure evil. "I see you have the fuzzy dog on Criminal Case."

He blinked some more, something he was doing a lot of tonight. "I had a fuzzy dog when Tommy was little, so it seemed like a good idea."

"Do you? What was his name?"

"Craig." At Wacey's incredulous look, TJ shrugged. "Thomas named him when he was wee."

"Craig. Craig the Dog." Wacey cackled. "I like it. We have all sorts here, you know—from Ring to Reisha to Bobblebutt."

"That and y'all have the oldest donkey known to man." *Crap.* "Is it okay for Dozer to be out? I can go put him in."

"Let's go get all the beasts where they belong. I bet most of them are in their stalls looking at the doors, willing them to close."

"You need to sit. I can do that."

"You suggesting I'm not the cowboy I used to be?"

"Not right now, no. This head bump is the least of your problems." The devil made him add, "You can pay me back and buy me supper."

"You driving? I'll take you to El Pinto."

"Craving nachos?" El Pinto was an Albuquerque institution, and they'd felt like it was such a long way to drive when they were teenagers.

"Do they still do the ones that are served with tongs?"

"Yep. Piled so high you can't see the plate at all." His belly rumbled, reminding him he'd been on his way home to eat. So TJ stole a grape.

"Cool. Austin is fab, but I miss home cooking."

"I bet." Texas and New Mexico had very different versions of Mexican food. Both good, but it all depended on what you grew up with.

"Dude, do you realize we've had a polite adult conversation for going on minutes?"

"I know. Should we snarl?" He chuckled a little.

"It's that or fuck like bunnies, man." Wacey's eyes went wide as saucers. "Oh. Oh, man. That was totally out of line. Sorry."

"It was utterly out of line since you can't back it up, asshat. Not nice to get me going." He would jack off like a fiend at home.

Wacey stared at him, obviously shocked as hell. "Well, shit."

He'd managed to make Wacey Bene speechless. Go him.

"What, you think I don't still want you, Wacey Bene? Because you'd be wrong." He turned his head and laid a hot one right on Wacey's mouth. Then TJ knew he had to run. "I'll get one of the hands to put the horses in."

"You are a bastard, Tank. I will pay you back for this."

"Will you? Promise?" He walked right out the door, kinda feeling on top of the world. He remembered that he had Dee's number from the other day. Dee would be discreet for Wacey.

This was going to be the most fun he'd had in years, at least if he played his cards right.

TJ figured it was a good thing he never lost at cards.

Chapter Nine

WACEY managed to not friend TJ online for three days, then couldn't put it off anymore. He was trapped in the house, and damn, he was bored.

Finally he hit the Friend button and waited.

It took maybe an hour before his friend request was accepted, and it drove him nuts enough that he thought about making a profile for Dozer just to see if TJ would accept that.

Thank God he didn't have to stoop that low.

Besides, TJ seemed to remember Dozer, so there was a definite level of awkward.

Not that awkward wasn't his middle name right now. Three life-threatening things in less than a month, and at least two of them seemed deliberate and aimed specifically at him.

Still, at least the folks didn't know, and he wasn't dealing with a full house all the time. Hell, give him another couple of weeks and he'd be driving. Therapy was going so much better. He wasn't gonna think about how seeing TJ had motivated him to do more and more all the time. How lame would that be?

Seriously.

He played a round of Criminal Case, checking his messenger over and over.

What are you up to, W? Popped up, and he almost dropped his iPad.

Thank God he was in his bed, and his tablet just slid on the pillow. *Resting after PT. U?*

Watching some weird shit on Netflix.

Yeah? What?

Was he doing this? Chatting with TJ the asshole?

Uh… It's called Haven *I think. Weird. Stephen King or something.*

Scary? He could hang with a periodic scary movie.

More mystery. I think. Save me from myself.

How did he answer that? *You want to call?*

I do. Need your number.

Well, okay. That was… kinda wonderful and strange. He sent it, because… oh hell. He'd blame it on the concussion.

The phone rang a lot faster than the friend request had been accepted.

"Hey, man. How goes?" See him. See him be cool and calm.

"I was bored to tears." TJ chuckled, a warm sound that took Wacey back years. He reminded himself that TJ was not interested in anything more than a hookup, if that. Who knows? Maybe the man was into teasing and got off on that. Regardless, he needed to watch himself.

"Yeah. I get that."

"I bet. You're used to going and doing. You're killed Criminal Case."

"Yeah. There's only so much random surfing a guy can do." He'd already burned through a dozen or more books this week.

"Uh-huh. Well, don't forget you owe me dinner. I'm off all day tomorrow."

"I'm still not cleared to drive, so you'd have to pick me up." Because that wouldn't be weird.

"What time? Take about half an hour to get there."

"Like I'm scheduled real tight these days." He had therapy twice a week, and then he waited for something to happen.

"Well, why don't we go early? Do lupper. Like three?"

"I can handle that. You going to come in your blue-light special?"

"Nah. I'm not even on call. I'll drive the pickup. I know you don't want to be seen with a cop," TJ teased, laughter clear in his voice.

"That's bad for rodeo trash like me."

"Hey, I've never had any beef with you rodeo assholes."

He found himself cackling like a big bird. "No?"

Wacey wasn't surprised. They were self-contained. That wasn't just his family's deal. Rodeo folks tended to stick together. Even worse, TJ had always been a townie.

A townie. What, in a town of five hundred people? They'd all ridden horses to school more than once, including Tank. God, he hadn't thought of that nickname in years, but it popped right out so easily.

"Nope. You deal with shit on your own. Rarely do you come into Turquoise and cause trouble."

"Occasionally at the bar…."

"Loula can take care of herself. She has a bat and a shotgun, and she looks like an old-fashioned prison matron. No cowboy on earth is gonna fight her."

"No. No. I heard that Tim and Derek tied it up in there one day and she damn near killed them."

"Yep. I stay outside her boundaries, in general. Now, if someone steals a truck or something, she calls me."

"Yeah. Yeah, Pop says that's bad these days."

"It is. The Chevy is a real commodity in Old Mexico, I reckon."

"I'll keep my Silverado in the garage, then."

"Good idea." TJ chuckled again. "Okay, Wace, I got to call my boys and tell them good night. Thanks for letting me call. I'll see you tomorrow at three."

"I'll be here." Because here was where he was.

"Don't pussy out on me, Wace."

Oh, asshole.

"Fuck you, Tank. Go call your children." He hung up, trying his best not to think. It wasn't a booty call. It wasn't anything. TJ had kids, a normal life.

It was supper.

Hell, he wasn't up to a booty call. Maybe a blowjob.

No. They were two old buddies reconnecting in the weirdest possible way, that was all.

Maybe it was more reconciling. Making up for past ugliness. How the fuck should he know?

He just rode horses and played Criminal Case.

At least until he could go back to work. He hoped to hell that eventuality came soon.

Chapter Ten

THE whole world was conspiring to keep TJ from his lupper date.

First Monica called him to pick up James from school because he'd spiked a fever at 102. Thank God Monica's mom was available to watch James, because as soon as he got the call to go get his kid, he also got a call from dispatch saying someone had almost drowned in the acequia. That was serious enough for him to make an appearance, even if he wasn't supposed to be working.

By 11:00 a.m., he was back in town, picking up the mail and checking in on Star Fassbender, because Angel Martinez said she'd had her painting vandalized.

"It's that bitch Ruth Ann and her psycho cult church people, Chief." Star was out there already, fixing it.

"I don't know, Star. Seems hard to get in here. Maybe a teenager."

"I'm putting up cameras."

"That's a sound idea. You can get a discount on home insurance."

"No one can see it from the street, TJ."

"Someone is stirring up trouble. I'll let Miz Ruth know so she can tell the church and they can all talk to their kids." He didn't look at his watch, but he wanted to.

"Where are you in such a hurry to go?" Star asked, her blue eyes twinkling.

"I have dinner plans."

"You're going out with Dub Bene, aren't you?"

"What?" He laughed when she made a face. "How do you even know that?"

"I have my ear to the ground, Chief."

"What else does the ground tell you, lady?"

"That it's been a long time since he's been home."

"It has. I missed him." That was the God's honest truth, even as badly as they'd parted. Wacey was still hot, funny, and amazing.

"I'll light a candle for you, then." She patted his cheek.

"Thanks." He thought he should thank her for that, at least. "Is there something I need to know?"

"I don't know, is there?"

"Star, I don't have time to play games. If there's something you want to tell me, tell me."

She looked up from under her sun hat. "Okay. Wacey Bene made a lot of changes when he took over the traveling company. Animal welfare, rider safety, modernizing. Some folks were none too happy. I say good on him, but it doesn't surprise me someone hurt him."

"What? Seriously? For making things better?"

"Better is, apparently, a matter of opinion." She gave him a gentle smile. "Change is hard for people, TJ. Some folks don't like new things." Star gestured at her mural.

"Star, honey, the Venus of Willendorf is an old, old thing."

She beamed at him, then. "She is! Did Monica teach you that?"

"No. My mom is an artist. You didn't know that?"

"I didn't. Is she in Santa Fe?"

"Taos."

"Oh, I would love to see her work."

"You would. She makes these great female power dolls." TJ chuckled. Dad was a cowboy and was now raising animals for all the Taos B and Bs.

"Oh Goddess! Honestly? Facebook? Tell me she has a Facebook!"

"She does. You got a paper?" He always had a pen in his pocket, but his notepads were all in the car.

"I have a phone."

"Techno pagan?"

"Indeed."

He laughed at her, but sure enough she tugged an iPhone out of her apron. "I'll put it on my Google Keep. What's her handle?"

"Mary Lynn Cook. M-a-r-y L-y-n-n."

"Rock on. I'll look her up."

"She'll be so tickled. They moved three years or so before you came to town."

"Up to the high country, huh?"

"She needed more space for her art, she said. Town was encroaching." TJ shook his head. Really, Dad had compromised by living on a five-acre property for years so she could sell art. He thought Mom had bought him twenty acres to pay him back in their semiretirement. It was possibly the most romantic thing he'd ever heard of.

He grinned at Star. "Anyway, if you want help installing cameras, holler at my office. I can come out Saturday." He really needed to get moving.

"Go. Go, you big dork. I can't wait to hear how it went!"

"Like I would tell you." He winked, knowing full well everyone in town would find out just how their date went.

She waved him off, and finally he was moving toward the ranch for the third time in his career.

He chuckled. The Bene Ranch had this mythical quality to his officers. Mike and Jack had been in awe that TJ had been allowed to search the main barn and the house.

He was going to milk that for weeks.

He didn't use the code that was set for law enforcement on the big gate; he just called Wacey. "Open the gate, man."

"Who is this?" Wacey's laughter was evident over the line.

"You want lupper or what, asshat?" He had to laugh along.

"Yeah, yeah." The line went dead, and then the gate opened, smooth as glass.

TJ pulled through, then wound down the road to the ranch, which was a hive of activity today. Last time it had been near deserted.

"Lord have mercy." He remembered this when he'd been not-dating Wacey, when he'd come down to the ranch to "hang out." Cowboys were either working, drinking, or sleeping.

He pulled into the parking area by the house, which had recently been regraded. He wondered if that had been for Wacey's wheelchair. Good thing the man was healing so well.

Wacey came down the ramp, moving slow and careful, the man in starched jeans and a snow-white button-down that had been pressed within an inch of its life.

That was hot as hell, that Wacey cared what he looked like for TJ, and he was sorry suddenly that his boots were all muddy from Star's garden. He stepped out of the truck, going around the front to see if Wacey needed help.

"Hey, Chief." Wacey tipped his head, the brim of that perfect straw 10X dipping down in greeting.

"Nope. I'm off duty, Wace." He grinned widely. "Now let's get out of here before someone proves me wrong."

Wacey snorted and headed out to his truck, the entire female cast of the Bene family watching them from the kitchen window.

TJ waved, because he refused to feel as if he didn't belong. He'd known those sisters of Wacey's all their lives, and Mrs. Bene was a nice lady who had always been good to him.

Mrs. Bene waved back and gave him a smile, but the girls just stared. Yeah.

He got the message.

TJ helped steady Wace when he climbed up into the truck. "You good?"

"I'm fine." Still, the sudden beads of sweat on Wacey's freshly shaved upper lip said maybe that had been a bit of a challenge.

He didn't argue. TJ just closed the passenger door and made his way back to the driver's seat. He would make sure the air was on cool, in case Wacey got queasy.

"Sorry I'm late. Someone grabbed me on the way out of town."

"No worries. I didn't have other plans."

"Ha-ha." He fiddled with the air. "Star had a little vandalism."

"Star… that the lady with the bright purple adobe?"

"Yep. She has a big Venus of Willendorf in her back garden. Someone spray painted fig leaves over her boobs and crotch." Maybe it had been Miz Ruth at that.

"Oh man. Folks need to not start a war with a witch."

"Right? I fully expect to see Star cursing people at the diner."

"I would pay to watch that. Do you remember when her name was Stacey and she was a band geek?"

"Lord. That makes me feel old."

"Well, if the foo shits."

"Oh, shut up. You weren't so tore up, I'd show you old. Butthead."

Wacey chuckled and shook his head. "Listen to you, Daddy-O."

"You are cruising for a bruising. I like it." Wacey had always been full of shit to bursting. Looked like that hadn't changed. TJ got a crooked grin, one gold tooth glinting at him.

"You still riding at all before this happened?" TJ asked, curious as hell about Wacey's life.

"I play safety man a lot, but I don't do a lot of roughstock anymore. I'm too damn busy."

"So tell me what all you're up to."

"Right now? I'm doing the planning for us, finding venues, schmoozing with city planners, things I can do on the computer or phone. It's helping Lacey out a ton."

"Yeah? Who's holding down the fort out in the show?" He got them rolling, amazed at how well they got along.

"Kacey. You remember him, yeah? For a just twenty-one-year-old kid, he's on it."

TJ sort of remembered Kacey, vaguely. The kid looked more like Lacey than Wacey—more like their Indios mama than their Anglo daddy. "I remember him—rhyming name number four. What was your mama thinking?"

"It was Daddy. It makes him laugh. Honestly, it's Sister, Macey, Dub, and Kace. That's what we're called mostly."

"Dub just doesn't suit you." He'd never called Wacey Dub, and Wacey had never called him TJ. Just Tank.

"So you've said." Wacey shrugged, and it was so weird, just one shoulder went up.

"You going to get better there? The shoulder, I mean."

"It has to. It's the worse of the hurts, I think. It's more sore, more stiff."

"Your leg is doing good?" The relief shouldn't be so great, really, but it was. TJ didn't want Wacey to be laid up.

"Yeah. Yeah, I mean, it's stiff, but honestly, it's going to be fine."

"Yay." They fell silent for a moment, Tim McGraw on the radio singing about humble and kind.

"You ever get to see him in concert, man?" Wacey asked.

"I did. He comes to Albuquerque sometimes, and I head down." He did love him some Tim McGraw.

"I went to Dallas a bunch to see him. He doesn't come to Austin, much."

"That seems weird, but I guess they have a different scene."

"I guess? I'm not there much. I travel all year round."

"You missing the road?" He hoped the answer was no, but he knew it was probably yes.

"I don't know. I worry about Kace, but I… I just don't know right now. I guess I do."

"Yeah." He bit off a hundred stupid responses. "I get it. Hell, I have a hard time getting up to Taos to see Mom and Dad."

"They finally moved up there, did they? Good on them."

"They did. They bought a B and B, then promptly turned it into a gallery and a farmstand, heritage meat place."

"Wow. That's… that's actually fucking cool, man."

"It really is." TJ thought his folks had a great life. "Your folks going to lay it down anytime soon?"

"Not a chance. Pop loves being the head of the universe, and right now he can be the head without doing too much physical work."

"He looks good." TJ hadn't seen Pop Bene in about two years, but he'd seemed hale and hearty the other day.

"He does. He's the cock of the walk."

He damn near swallowed his tongue. "You're evil. No one's dad needs to be associated with cock."

"Me? You're the one with the dirty mind, sir."

"I always have had one, especially when it comes to you." The drive up to the old 4th Street area of Albuquerque took less time than he'd thought. The time of day let them slip past the teeth of traffic for lunch and beat the early rush of people getting off work.

"It's funny—everything's different and exactly the same."

"Right? It's grown up a lot, but you get back here at El Pinto, and it's like going back in time."

"I think Austin changes every time I crawl back home."

"It's one of the fastest growing cities in the country, huh? The Burque not so much." TJ parked, and they could smell pinyon smoke and red chile as soon as they opened the doors.

Wacey eased himself out of the truck, and carefully made his way across the uneven dirt parking lot.

TJ didn't insult the man by offering an arm. His daddy was a cowboy; he knew better. He did stay close in case Wacey needed him, and he walked slow. And if he took a couple long stares at that teeny cowboy butt? So be it.

"Sorry, it takes me a while."

"I'm not in any hurry now. I was when I was running late to see you." Was that sappy? "Besides I like the view just fine."

"Are you flirting with me because I'm safe, man?"

"What?" TJ stopped and stared, and a man coming out of the restroom almost plowed into him since it was right by the door. "Sorry."

"No falling. My hands are full of crutches."

"Right. I'm sorry if I'm out of bounds." Wacey was never safe. Not ever.

"I didn't say that. I just want to know whether you're just queer-baiting."

"Queer…." Oh. Hello, that was an awful question. "Do you really think I would do that? I'm gay, Wacey. Always have been." He'd made peace with that, and he thought Monica had forgiven him.

"Tank, you have two babies and an ex-wife."

"I do." He chuckled. "Two, please." TJ waited until they were seated to keep talking, which was a feat in itself, because they ended up in the back forty. "Honey, I wanted so bad to be like everyone else. I needed to fit in. I'm sure some therapist somewhere would blame my mom and her naked goddess dolls, but really, I wanted to be a cowboy like my dad more than anything on earth."

"I know, Tank. You were very clear. I understand."

"No, you don't." He leaned his elbows on the table. "I sucked at it."

"I'm not sure what you want me to say."

He sat back and shrugged. "I don't. I just wanted you to know. Monica and I split because I came out to her. She deserved more. So did you. I was shitty." He paused, studying Wacey some. "But if I'm making you uncomfortable, I'll just leave it well enough alone."

"You're fine, man. I hear you. Do you eat guacamole?"

"I do." He loved guac. "You must if you're asking."

"I do. It's good back in Austin, but this is better."

"It is." Now he wasn't sure what to say. He hadn't been flirting hard, even, so now he felt constrained to polite, meaningless stuff. "You still okay with me salting the chips?"

"Yeah. Look, man. I wasn't trying to make you scared. I'm cool. Seriously."

"I'm not baiting you, Wace. I swear. I missed my best friend."

"Okay, then. We're clear. We'll all just be normal people, right?"

Seemed to him like Wacey Bene wasn't any bigger on emotional nonsense now than he was then.

"Sounds good." TJ had to grin. "So, who's trying to kill you?"

"I don't think anyone is. I think I had an accident, and now there's someone messing with the barns. Maybe they buried drugs in there or something."

"That would be the best answer, I guess. You can't think of anyone at all, though?" He hated to harp on it, but he was a cop. He didn't believe in coincidence.

Wacey looked at him and gave him another one-armed shrug. "I mean, I'm the boss, right? At least as far as the guys on the road go. You can't be the boss without pissing people off."

"Anyone you fired or anything?" He was checking off all the usual questions before moving on to harder ones.

"Sure. Dozens. I've been doing this ten years."

"What's the best part about your job?"

Wacey started to laugh, the sound rich and deep and sort of wonderful. "You want the honest answer or the professional answer?"

"The honest one, as long as it doesn't involve play-by-play of blowjobs or something."

"I love the horses. That's the best part. The horses and the people that understand them, like Kace." Wacey rolled his eyes but smiled. "I swear, it's stupid, but the truth. Being on the road is hard, but I got my brother and Dawson, and that's all I need. You ever seen Dawson?"

"No. Who's Dawson?" A tiny spurt of jealousy went through him, even if he didn't have the right to it.

"Here. I'll show you. He's the love of my life." Wacey chuckled and grabbed his phone, showing the wallpaper of a black Arabian with a white star on its forehead.

"Oh. He's gorgeous. Seriously. I have ponies for the boys and two quarter horse paint mixes I ride, but he's something." TJ put all the emotions riding him away to explore later.

"Kace is taking care of him right now. He'll bring Dawson back to me in a few weeks."

"That's awesome." Did that mean Wacey might stay a bit?

"Yeah. I talked to the doctor, and they're not going to release me this season, for sure, and I'm not sure what my immediate plans are."

"Oh, well, I bet your folks have plenty for you to do." *No dancing, TJ.*

"Like I said, I'm pulling stuff off Lace's plate. She's preggers, you know, so she'll need to back off a little, especially if God has a sense of humor and blesses her with another set of twins."

"Twins. I see them in town every so often, and I think, thank God mine are a few years apart."

"Those boys are hellions. Derek has them chained up in the casita at night, I swear." Wacey still had the best shit-eating grin on earth. "They're eight and a half, and together that makes them teenagers, you know."

"I do. Together mine are a tween, and that's hard enough."

"How old are yours again? I hadn't even known you had kids."

Now that was a shock. He knew the Benes—hell, he sat on a bunch of committees with Pop Bene, and Monica and Lacey and Derek all went to the same church. Macey Bene was a legend with her brood and bright red hair. Someone ought to have said.

"Six and four. Thomas is the older, James the little one." He loved them so. "They make me nuts, but they're good kids."

"Good deal. You always wanted normal, so good on you."

"I told you I sucked at it, right?" TJ shook his head wryly. "Now, sharing them with Monica and Monica's mom? That works for me."

Wacey looked like he didn't have the slightest idea what the fuck to say. "I'm tickled for you, honey."

"I guess it was a shock, huh? Why the hell didn't anyone tell you?"

"The girls said they thought it would just hurt my feelings that you moved on. It wasn't like I intended to come home."

"Oh." Huh. He'd ponder that one later.

"You folks ready to order?" Their waitress had been back and forth with water and chips and salsa. Now she was poised, pen over her pad of paper.

"Green chile chicken enchiladas, please ma'am, and a side of guacamole."

"You got it. And for you?" She glanced at TJ.

"Uh." Okay, he was caught. "Half-size nachos, please."

"Hell, just change it to one full-sized and we'll share. Keep the guac, though."

"You got it." She marked out something and scribbled and smiled. "I'll have that right out."

TJ chuckled. "The nachos are still huge."

"Fucking A. I've still got a hollow leg."

"Good deal. Guess you didn't get old like me, huh?" That still stung a little.

"Uh… I have lost ten teeth, broken my neck once, both arms, both legs, a collarbone, every finger, both ankles, and every rib. I may be the living definition of old cowboy."

"You're still skinny as a rail." TJ grinned. He could eat a goodly bit too, so why was he so grumpy?

"I am. We all are, huh? I guess that's just pure genetics because the girls never go on about dieting and shit, but Tim and Derek sure as shit do."

"Do they? That makes me feel better." He tried the salsa, which made his eyes water. "Someone was mad today."

"You are still a lightweight, huh, or is it really warm?"

"I am not a lightweight! I'm New Mexican, man."

"Uh-huh…." Wacey coughed out a "Pussy man."

"You try it and tell me." TJ would have poked Wacey for that, but the man was injured.

Wacey scooped up a huge bite with a chip, humming as he chewed. "That is nice sauce, Tank."

"Asshat. Your entire soft palate could be melting and you would lie."

"You know it." And did Wacey look guilty? No. Not at all.

TJ grabbed another chip, just going easier on the salsa. It was bright and yummy, and his tongue burned.

They ate in silence, watching each other like they were enemies.

It was the waitress who broke their long stare, because she came bearing nachos. "You want more salsa?"

"Please, thank you." Wacey finally smiled at him. "You look just the same, you know. I keep looking for proof you haven't got the picture of Dorian Gray hidden somewhere."

"You said I was old." He tried not to puff up with pride.

"You have kids. That totally makes you older than me." Wacey winked at him. "I was surprised. I didn't know about the kids. I wasn't ready to see you yet."

"I get that. I had heard you were back in town, but it never occurred to me you'd show up in town in a wheelchair. I know your pride."

"I was on my way back from the doctor's. Macey suggested breakfast."

"Ah." TJ felt like a jerk about that day, so he moved on. "You look better every day."

"I'm working hard enough that I ought to. Soon I'll be more mobile and life will get easier for everyone." Wacey pulled some chicken out of the nachos, mixed it with some crema.

"Did you want the enchiladas, man?" He didn't want Wacey thinking he couldn't pay his share if he was tapped out.

"Huh? There's no way I can eat this and enchiladas! This is the size of a pickup bed!"

"True." *Oh, good.* TJ felt a little like he was in a minefield, trying to figure out where to step. It was like having some stranger living inside your best friend or something.

"I'm just trying for the perfect bite, you know? The absolutely right one."

TJ shook his head, and suddenly his shoulders relaxed down from around his ears. This was Wacey. The Wacey he knew. A little goofy, a lot OCD, and fiercely protective of both those facts.

He settled in to munch, his heart lighter, his head clearer.

Wacey's phone rang, and he frowned. "Pop. You mind if I grab this?"

"Nope." No way was he gonna tell a man not to talk to his daddy.

"Hey, Pop. Hmm? I'm on the Westside." Wacey stopped, and then his head tilted like a pup hearing a whistle. "What? What the fuck do you mean?"

TJ went on alert. In fact, he waved over their server. "Can you get us a box, please?"

"No. No way. I'll be right there. Give me forty-five minutes. I'm coming. No, Pop, I don't know what the fuck is going on!" Wacey clicked the phone closed, face gone all thunderclouds. "I have to go."

"What's going on?" He slipped the server his card when she came back with the box.

"Someone put poisoned feed under my window. Mama went out there and found a bunch of dead birds. One of the dogs is at the vet's now. What the actual fuck?"

"What?" TJ scribbled his name on the check and tucked away his card. "Shit. They need to leave it there, man, even if they have to put chicken wire over it."

"What? Why? They've got to get it away from the critters. They took some to the vet." Wacey stood up and damn near went ass over teakettle.

"I know, but we have to find out who's doing it. At least save me some to send to the state lab." TJ shoveled nachos into the box. "Don't you fall."

"I won't. Let me call home." Wacey braced himself on one of the low chairs and grabbed his phone again.

TJ got the rest of their food and his hat, waiting for Wacey, who couldn't walk and call at the same time.

"Yeah. Yeah. No! No, I didn't hear a damn thing last night. I took a pain pill and crashed." Wacey grimaced, clearly in pain. "TJ wants to preserve the scene. Barring that, he needs a big baggie of the feed."

Good man. He waited for Wacey to hang up and start moving out the crazy warren of rooms that made up the restaurant.

"You need help?" he asked, knowing Wacey wanted to move fast. "I can go get the truck if you can be steady enough to get to the door."

"Go." Wacey jerked his chin toward the front, and TJ sprinted outside.

Poisoned feed outside Wacey's window? Seriously? This wasn't some random asshole with a barn fetish. No way.

No fucking way.

Chapter Eleven

"I SWEAR to God, Wacey Bene! If Ring dies because of you!" Lacey was sobbing, screaming before he even got out of the truck.

He didn't bother to answer her. He just started walking over toward the side of the house, lurching like the world's newest zombie, heading toward the gaggle of cowboys keeping anything off the pile of shit under his window. TJ followed him, and the man was like a barrier between him and Lace. Wacey got it. Ring was her dog, and she would fight a lion for him.

"What did you think you were doing? Poisoned feed?"

At that, he stopped still, one hand curling into a fist. Pardon him? He loved these critters. Always had. Always would. Not to mention, it would take him and a wagon to get this much feed out here. He couldn't even walk right no more, for fuck's sake. "Get your ass into the house," he snapped.

"Don't you boss me—"

"Now!" he roared, and the whole world went silent for a long second.

She stared at him, her eyes huge and wet in her pale face. Then she turned tail and ran.

"Wow," Tank muttered. "That was cool."

"Don't. I have to make myself heard." He was the littlest of all of them, and he had to deal with the most stubborn breed of human on earth every goddamn day.

"She thinks you did it, man? Why would she think that?" TJ's voice was carefully without inflection. *Cop voice*, Wacey thought. Christ, seriously? He didn't need this shit. He hadn't brought this here. He hadn't. He was just here to recover, and then he'd get the hell out of Dodge.

"I don't know. Go ask her." He didn't have time for this bullshit. Right now he had to figure out what the fuck happened and fix it. "What the fuck, Martin? Seriously. Is it from our barns? Has someone checked the rest of the feed? Is there a trail? Who found it? Pop said Mama came out to do something?"

"Sí. Buñuelos. She had them for us."

"Okay. Okay. What else?"

"No trail, señor. Swept clean."

"Well, fuck a duck sideways. That takes effort."

TJ was staring at him a little, and he rolled his eyes. *Whatever.* He couldn't talk on his phone and walk, for fuck's sake. How dare anyone suspect him? The bastard was so caught up in the fact that there was an openly gay man in town that he was thinking with his nutsac.

If Wacey had entertained any thought of them really hooking up, today had proved it was a stupid idea. Tank was wanting to have a little flirtation, to prove that Wacey still wanted a piece of him.

There was nothing more to it, and now Tank was thinking he was a criminal to boot.

Fucker. This was not his motherfucking fault.

"Can someone get me a gallon bag?" TJ asked, and one of the cowboys ran off to make it happen.

"As soon as the chief is done, I want y'all to shovel this up and then put it in a galvanized can. One with a lid. I got to figure out how to dispose of it. Are there men looking for tainted feed in the barns?"

Martin nodded. "Tim, Derek, and El Jefe with the others."

"Let me call the state and see what they suggest." TJ stepped aside, pulling out his sleek smartphone.

Red Hollister shook his head, the world-champion bulldogger massive now that he'd retired. "I don't get it, Dub. What the actual fuck?"

"My sentiments exactly. Like I'd hurt the critters."

"Eh, don't stress that, Dub." Derek came jogging up, damn near bowling him over. "My girl's just hormonal as fuck. Doc called. Ring's going to be fine. He'll stay overnight, just to be safe, but he'll make it."

"Oh, good." He tried to cross himself and damned near toppled.

TJ came back and began taking pictures. "State says to send them a sample, and they suggest containing it until you can incinerate it safely away from animals and people."

"You heard the chief, y'all. Get a move on. Baggie of this evil shit for him, then let's take it and burn it. Martin, listen to me, man. Tell the new men, none of y'all roast any meat over this crap, okay? It will make you sick as dogs."

"Sí, Señor Dub. I tell them." Martin nodded hard.

"You rock, man." Martin had been with them so long that Wacey couldn't remember the man's solid presence not being on the ranch.

Wacey hoped he could be that one day. The solid presence.

"Not very much! Too busy." Martin just laughed and laughed, because he'd bought a rocking chair to put on the porch of his new casita last year and said he never got to use it.

Wacey grinned and nodded, and then Mama was there with a lawn chair for him. "Mijo! You have to sit down before you fall down."

"I'm fine, Mama. You calm Sister down?"

"No. But she's not going to beat you down anymore, so it's fine."

"I'd like to see her try. She accused me of doing this, Mama. Me. She is officially on my shit list."

"She's just scared, mijo. She had no idea what to do."

He looked at his mama, trying hard not to snarl. "Periodically it would be nice if someone would pretend that I'm not the only responsible child in this family."

"Fuck off, Dub." Macey was right there, popping up like cholla in the desert, staring him down, that grin playing on her face.

"What? It's true. Functional. Responsible."

"Tired." TJ chuckled. "That's all that responsibility stuff gets you. Tired."

"No shit." And he was—tired, that is. "I'm gonna call Pop and see where they need me."

"I'll need to talk to everyone," TJ murmured. "Can you set up a room for me at the house?"

"Sure. Also, if you're asking, I've fought more than a few men and might have put my fist through a wall, but I've never once hit a woman, and I've never hurt an animal."

"Wacey, I know you didn't do this." Tank stared right at him, and he stared back.

"You didn't." And that was what mattered. Tank had doubted him for that split second; he'd seen it. He didn't need that shit. "I'll go set you up something."

"Thanks." TJ said it softly, and Wacey wanted to growl.

He didn't, but he sure as shit wanted to.

When he clumped in, Lacey was sitting in the kitchen, all red-eyed and wet-cheeked, and she opened her mouth and got out, "Dub."

He lifted one hand. "Not one more fucking word, Sister. You and me? Right now we are not friends. You sit there and you keep your motherfucking mouth shut against me."

She swallowed hard, fire flashing in her eyes. "No, I will not. I'm sorry, and I was out of line, but what the hell is going on around here?"

"You tell me."

"What?"

"Well, you sure as shit think I know. Why shouldn't I believe you do?" He had exactly as much idea as anyone else.

"Because it all started when you came back?"

That was true enough, he guessed. Maybe. Who the fuck knew?

"Fine." If it was him, he'd get his ass back on the road. "Chief needs a room set up to question people, please."

She slapped the last of the tears from her cheeks. "I can do that. Sit down before you fall down, butthead."

"Thank you." He headed for his room and packed his go bag, then sat on the edge of his bed for a second, hurting so bad spots flashed before his eyes. Adrenaline only made it so far.

"Are you okay, mijo?" His mom had followed him up, and she frowned when she saw his bag.

"I'm fine, Mama."

"You're not leaving."

"I have to get the fuck out of here."

"Watch your mouth. You're not leaving. You just came home to me!"

"Mama, I can't be where people who say they love me accuse me of poisoning dogs. I just can't. I ain't like that." He didn't belong here. He hadn't for a long time. "I'm going back to work. I been off long enough."

"Kacey is doing okay, mijo. Please." She sat next to him. "I know it hurts. I'm sorry."

"Everything hurts, Mama." His whole world. His fucking soul.

"Of course it does. You need to rest. Really rest. Not run around and get hit. Maybe we should send you to a hotel."

"Nonsense." That was Macey. "I vote we hit Lace with a shovel."

"Okay. Hit Tank too?"

"You want me to kick him off the property?" Mama asked. She could be fierce.

The temptation to say yes was huge, but that was his heart talking. "Nah. I'm just… worn. He's a cop. He has to look at all the stuff."

"So you rest. Me and Mama will deal with this shit."

"Okay. Promise?" He wanted to sleep. Just sleep.

"Dub, I will fucking rip the throat out of anyone that bothers you."

He did love Macey. Lace too. Just not right now.

"Thank you." He would just lie down and forget the world for a bit. Especially TJ Cook.

That man had issues, and he didn't have the heart for that shit anymore.

TJ sat across from Monica, his eyes on his coffee, which was really because he was about to doze off, not because he didn't want to look at her. Her mom had the boys, and they were having their biweekly planning session. She had a planner. With color-coded stickers.

Seriously.

It was ridiculous and cute as hell, all at the same time. Sort of like Minions. His boys loved those banana guys.

"Are you listening to me, TJ?"

"Nope." He said it cheerfully. "I was thinking which Minion you are. Not Bob. More Kevin."

"I am Dr. Nefario, no question."

He thought about that. "Yes. Yes, you are. Okay. So, I have to ask you something."

"Ask away, honey. You look like shit."

"Tired." He did meet her gaze now. "So all this shit is happening at the Bene Ranch. Someone mentioned maybe Wacey was doing it. For attention. I know that's utter bullshit, but I got to tell you, when I asked him why Lacey thought it was his fault, he sure got his back up."

"Wouldn't surprise me, I guess. He's used to a lot on the road and now he's bored and stuck at home. I got to say, though, I'd be asking about the difference between 'did he do it' and 'is this his fault.'"

"Yeah? You think someone would self-destruct like that? Like not in a movie?" He wanted an opinion from someone who'd never been as far in Wacey's back pocket as he'd been.

"Sure. Happens all the time. He's used to living on the road, an exciting, high-stress job, and suddenly he's having to be Jimmy Stewart a la *Rear Window*. Makes perfect sense." There was a hint of hesitation in her voice.

"But?" he asked.

"Well, it's like I said before, Wacey Bene loves that rodeo company. If you saw worry there, or maybe guilt, I'm thinking it's because he knows this is his fault."

"Hmm." He sipped his coffee. "That jives more with the Wacey I know."

"The one you broke up with to marry me?" she teased, not quite gently.

"Wasn't his fault. Or yours." He shrugged. TJ tried hard to take responsibility for his mistakes. He adored Monica and never regretted having her in his life.

"No, but how badly is he hurt? Is he depressed? Suicidal? Is he practicing self-harm? You may have to call in psych services as the authorities." Now she was just baiting him.

"He's bad enough he had to go back to the hospital after the first attack in the barn. I don't know. I just—okay, so what if someone is trying to hurt him?" Time to just focus on the situation that actually made sense.

"Then you have to catch them, because that's bad."

He always bounced his cases off Monica. Always. "How do I find out who it is?"

"Well, you could have him interviewed, but that would be weird."

"A little, yeah."

"You could ask him to leave?"

"This is his home, honey. Also he's hurt and not the bad guy." Not to mention he didn't want Wace to just up and go again.

"Hrm. It's more fun to do this with robbers. Surveillance?"

Now there was an idea. He could do some of it himself, maybe call in an off-duty buddy or two from the Burque. That would help keep Wacey safe from a perp too.

"Either that or you can tie him up and leave him in the barn."

"Don't tempt me. I want him to rest. Get better."

Her lips twisted. "How is he? I mean, seriously. Scary hurt?"

"He's not scary, no. He's healing up, but he keeps getting hit over the head, or running after loose donkeys."

"Loose donkeys. Lord have mercy. So how did lunch go? Are you still chatting on Facebook?"

"We were. I think he's mad at me." TJ sighed. "He thought I was treating him like a suspect. Maybe I was a little, fuck if I know. I wasn't trying to. Hell, I didn't even interview him because he fell asleep. Now he's ignoring my texts."

"Like on the phone or Facebook, because on the Facebook, you can tell if he's read them at all."

"On the phone. I'll PM him." He grinned at her. "Split a cinnamon roll with me, and I'll look at your planner."

"Thank you for bowing to glance at it." She nodded for him, though, and winked.

"What? Have I ever not just let you tell me what to do?"

"Shut up. Tommy starts summer reading club this week."

"Rock on." He loved that. TJ loved reading with his kids, and Tommy was still so happy to sit and do stuff like that. James was slower to focus, but it took time to understand books didn't mean bedtime.

"I'm so glad you enjoy that, because the library is having a big kickoff party, and I'm on shift."

"Oh ho! I like that. That was sneaky. Talented, but sneaky."

She grinned like a Cheshire cat. "I'm the mom."

"You are that. Is James signed up too?" Like James didn't do something Tommy was doing.

"He is, but he's more interested in soccer."

Soccer. "When does that start?" Shit, that and hockey were the only sports he didn't know all the rules to, wasn't it?

"I have him in a noncompetitive thing. You know, informal, no stress, just kick the ball?"

"Can't we have them in the same things?"

"If one wasn't a reader and the other wasn't a runner, maybe."

They said runners ended up not getting picked for football and became loners. He didn't want James to be a serial killer later in life, so maybe she was right. A kid needed to learn how to be on a team.

"At least they both love horses, huh?"

"They do. And four-wheelers. And each other."

She grinned at him. "That they do."

"What else? Doctors? Bakers? Candlestick makers?"

"James has a physical for said soccer, but I have that. They both want to go to Ruidoso with their Gran at some point this summer. You know how much they love it."

"I do. How are you, honey?"

"Tired, but happy. I love my life, you know."

He studied her, deciding in moments she meant it. Thank God. He did worry someday she'd get tired of Turquoise and move off to Santa Fe or something. Or worse, Colorado.

"Stop it, TJ. I wouldn't take your boys from you. We're in this together, right?"

"We are. I know I'm an ass." She told him weekly not to doubt her. He didn't. He really didn't. He was a cop. It was his job to worry about everything.

"You totally are. So, what are you going to do about your ex?"

"Have breakfast with her?" He waggled his brows.

"I'm just the mother of your children. I'm talking about the real ex." Evil woman.

"I have no idea. He's too laid up to screw the truth out of him, and he's too stubborn to sit and talk with. I don't think he's doing this. I think someone is doing it to him. Because of him. All these years as law enforcement and I never had one call to the Bene Ranch."

"Oh, a real mystery. Did he have a boyfriend? A rival? Maybe it's one of the other kids?"

"I thought about Lacey. She's preggers, and you of all people know how crazy pregnant women are." He winced ahead of time, knowing she would kick him.

Yep. Damn her aim.

"I'll see what's what when I see it, I guess." TJ hated being out of control of the situation.

"You should poke him. Tell him to quit pouting. Make him tell you what's up."

"Maybe I will. It never worked with you."

She snorted. "I'm not a man. If I'm pouting, you ought to know why without asking."

"Right…. No wonder we broke up."

"We broke up because you're a fudge packer and you wanted to be a cop. I did get two gorgeous boys out of it, though."

"I paid for your college…."

"That too. Also, I like your mom."

"She likes you better than me." He cut the cinnamon roll in half. "Okay, lay the rest of the planner on me." Roses and words. Those were her stickers this week. Words strung together into phrases like *Have the best week ever*.

Ridiculous, but they made her smile, and she always knew where the boys needed to be and when, so he just had to take pictures of that damn thing on his phone.

He snapped a few in fact, listening to her tell him all about James and buying shin guards.

Really, they could just learn to rope, couldn't they? That was something.... Maybe he could take them to rodeo school for part of the summer. The Benes had a pee wee camp.

Oh, there was an idea and a half....

His boys, access to Wacey—he liked it.

He would look into the schedule. Then he would put it on Monica's calendar.

He'd even give her cowboy stickers.

She would probably kick him again when he did, but hey, he would owe her for letting the boys do something so hardy. Not dangerous. It was culturally relevant and shit.

He grinned at Monica when she gave him the stank eye. She had an amazing spider sense.

"Be good, you. Whatever you're thinking about."

"I am good. Very good." He winked. "Nothing to worry about."

"Uh-huh." She shut the planner and put it in the fancy bag that held it.

"You heading out?" She always had a million errands to run on her days off, but he treasured their time.

"Nope. I just thought we could visit. I've got another hour for you."

"That's awesome. I should have gotten more cinnamon rolls." In another hour, he could have eaten three.

"Did you want another one?"

"God, yes." He was starving.

"I'll go get one and another coffee. You're okay?"

"I'm good, Moni. Thanks." He smiled, watching her order and chat with the barista. She did love her weird coffee.

Sometimes he wished.... But if wishes were horses, beggars would ride.

He was who he was, and lying about it hurt both of them. Being honest, they were closer than ever before.

She came back, and he made a point to talk about her, not work, and only tangentially, the boys. She'd carved out this time for him. Soon she was packing up, leaning over to kiss his cheek. "Don't forget that the boys are with your mom, not mine."

"I won't. I'll pick them up after my shift." Unless they called and begged to stay with Granny. It happened at least once a week.

That was fine with him. That was a haul up to his mom, even if she met him halfway, and he had some things to think about.

"I'll see you Sunday!"

"Good deal, honey."

TJ stretched, stood, then went to get in line. He really needed to get one more pastry to go.

Someone came in, stood altogether too close to him, and he checked the shadow. "Hey, Josh."

"Howdy, Ossifer. You're dating Dub? Seriously?"

"Shut up."

"You didn't even call. We're totally jealous."

"Shut up."

"I'll buy your pastry if you come to the house and dish. My girl is burning up for gossip and a croissant."

He pondered, but not very long. He could use a long chat. "It's a deal, but you're buying my coffee too."

Chapter Twelve

"DUDE, seriously? You look like shit."

Wacey blinked across the room, trying to figure out whose voice that was, because it sounded like….

Whoa.

"Really, Peter? You got no room to talk."

The man looked like a skinny, tall Sasquatch, dreads down to his waist, wearing a pair of cutoffs tied with a piece of rope, but those bright eyes—one blue and one green? Those belonged to one man, his best friend from high school, Peter Nunn.

"At least mine's a political decision." Peter ducked into Wacey's bedroom carrying a bag and a cup from the diner. "I brought you a milkshake and a bacon sandwich. Your mom said to just come on in and find you."

"Did she call you?" Mama was starting to get a little hysterical.

"Yep. Said you were dying and I had to come out of the studio and see for myself."

"Your voicemail said you were up in the mountains."

"Yep. Now I'm back, and I never listen to voicemails."

He took the milkshake and sat up. "That's why I didn't leave one."

"Yeah, well, here I am." Peter pulled two sandwiches out of the bag, handed him one, then sat on his bed to munch the other. "Not much changed in here."

"I haven't been here in ten years. You've changed."

The Peter he remembered had been a goofy, cheery little guy. This was… wow. He guessed you went one way or the other in Turquoise. Cowboy and law-abiding or artsy and subversive.

Wacey could use a little subversive in his life.

"I just came out of every closet, cowboy." Peter chuckled softly. "You did that too, way before me."

"I only had the one."

"Yeah. Still, you were my hero."

Wacey blinked over at Peter. "Thanks, man. It's good to know."

Right now he needed to believe that.

"Uh-huh. After we eat, you're getting your ass out of bed and into the shower. Your mom tells me you haven't been to therapy or anything. Wallowing is stupid."

"I'm not wallowing!" Much. He'd been exhausted, but he had to admit, he was bored.

"Uh-huh. Then you have no beef with getting up and showering."

"If my legs will work."

"I'll help. Upsey-daisy."

"Let me finish my damn sandwich, you nut!" He was a little hungry, after all.

"Oh!" Peter looked down at the sandwich he still held. "I ought to eat too."

"How much weed have you smoked, man?"

"Not enough, Dub. Nowhere near enough."

"What happened, man?" Something had to have, right? Pete was so changed.

"Life. Art. I tried to be something I wasn't, and it didn't work."

What the hell did that mean? Wacey shook his head. "You're not going to tell me the whole sordid tale?" Pete used to be able to just ramble for hours.

"Nope. I have left it behind me. Hopefully in a flooded arroyo."

Wacey gave Peter the greasy eyeball. "You're like reading an Umberto Eco book."

"Oh man. I'm impressed you can read a day sheet…."

"Yeah, yeah. I'm impressed you know what a day sheet is."

Peter chortled. "Remember that summer I came to rodeo school? I was trying to get your attention away from TJ."

Yeah, that hadn't worked. Not even when they were teenagers. "I remember. You hurt your wrist and freaked."

"I sucked at it. I was scared I would never jack off again."

"Yeah, and at fifteen, that's a thing."

Peter snorted. "Shit, at damn near thirty it's a thing."

"You think so? I guess I haven't felt up to it." Wacey blinked. "That was good, huh? You know, *felt up*? Get it?"

"Lord love a duck, you are a dipshit." For a second, Peter sounded as cowboy as they came.

"I am." Wacey grinned. "It's good to see you, man."

"Ditto. So did you really have lunch with TJ?"

"I did. El Pinto. The food was great." Hell, the company had been good too, up until afterward.

"Uh-huh. I sense conflict."

"What would we have to be conflicted about?" Wacey sighed. "He thinks I'm the one causing trouble around here, poisoning animals, hurting myself. I just know it."

"Huh. That's weird." Pete waggled his eyebrows. "I mean, he should know you'd rather mutilate him than yourself."

"Bitch." That's not what he wanted. Not even a little.

"So, make him apologize so you can get over it."

"There's nothing he has to apologize for. He's a cop. I'm a suspect." And that was safer for them both.

"You're still pouty." Peter licked his fingers. "That was good bacon."

"Shouldn't you hippie types be vegan?"

"Fuck off, rodeo man. I will beat you to death with a pork chop."

"Haiiiya! Kung fu pork!" Wacey cackled at their old joke, laughing until his ribs hurt.

"You know it. Take your milkshake, get a shower, and then we'll go sit in front of a television and make faces at each other."

"I can probably do that."

"I await your get-off-your-assedness." Pete gave him a slight one-armed hug, then helped him up, wincing at his legs. "Jesus, Dub. What happened?"

"Horses panicked. I don't know, man. I didn't hurt them. I swear to God."

"Dub, no one has ever accused you of being cruel to a horse."

"Lacey accused me of poisoning the dog."

Pete whistled low. "Well, that's what you get for becoming a stranger."

He stopped and stared. "I was working. For them."

A stranger. Was that it? Some random local pissed someone new was in town? Did that happen?

"I know that, doof, but Turquoise has grown. Your family has grown. Has TJ looked at your brother-in-law?"

"Derek?" No. Derek was one of them.

"What about Tim?"

"What about him? I mean, he likes to go to the casinos." Wacey had been the one to introduce Derek and Lace, and Tim was the shop teacher at the middle school, for fuck's sake.

"I just mean it could be anyone. If you coming back threatened their existence."

"Okay." *But who? And why? And what the fuck?*

"You never know about people. I swear it wasn't me if TJ asks."

"Would he ask?" God, his head hurt.

"Go shower. I'll stand at the door and protect you."

"Fucker." He trudged to the bathroom, resisting the urge to sit on the toilet. Shower. Then he could huddle on the couch with Pete.

God, he needed to shave. He needed to get out of bed and find a horse and ride.

He ran the water until it steamed, then stepped in, grateful for the bars Pop had put in all the bathrooms a few years ago.

By the time he got out and dressed, he doubted Peter was still waiting. He walked by his room, and someone had already changed his sheets for him.

"Thanks, Mama. You rock."

"Peter is waiting for you in the den. I think he missed you."

"He looks different, doesn't he?"

Mama snorted. "That is a terrible understatement."

"Yeah. It's…."

Mama patted his shoulder. "Please. Your Pop and Rusty are entertaining him."

"Oh God."

Rusty was a rodeo clown, and bless his heart, he was a little past his prime jokewise.

Mama rolled her eyes. "Aiieee. Right? Come on as soon as you get dressed."

Right. A robe wasn't gonna do it.

"You know it." Sweats and a T-shirt would have to be enough. He couldn't manage jeans. No one would care.

He dressed slowly after Mama left, then slid his feet into slippers. God, just that had him wheezing.

He had to get in better shape. Had to….

What the fuck was that sound?

There was a rustling noise. Coming from his closet.

He frowned, grabbed his crutches, and moved toward the partially open door. He peered in without touching, but he couldn't see anything. "We got mice? Bella, is that you?"

Mom's damned Himalayan managed to sneak in all sorts of places.

He reached with his crutch, opened the door wider, shocked as shit when a friggin' rattler came into view. He fought to keep his balance. He didn't want to go down in front of the snake.

"Fuck. Pop! Bring the pistol!"

Pop thundered down the hall. "I have the .22. What is it, son?"

"Rattler in my closet. You be careful. He's a doozy!"

"Holy shit!" That came from the door, where Peter stood, eyes wide.

Rusty peered over Peter's shoulder, but the man was terrified of snakes, so there was no way he was getting any closer.

"Y'all? Hello? Gun?"

"Don't you let him get blood on my floor!"

He rolled his eyes. For fuck's sake. Then he hit the snake with his crutch.

"Is anyone going to help the crippled guy?"

Pop whacked the thing with the butt of the .22 rifle, crushing its head. "Woo."

"Nicely done, Pop."

"You'd stunned it."

"Y'all are a great team." Rusty's tone was pretty damned sarcastic.

"Almost like family." Pete's voice was dry as dust.

"Shut up and go get a trash bag." Mama whacked Pete hard.

"Are you gonna cook it for supper, Mama?"

"I will beat you, mijo."

"Make great burritos," Pop said.

"Viejo, I will beat you too. Get it out of my house. I will go make Bloody Marys."

"Rock on! Mama Bene's Bloody Marias!" Peter came back with the bag, bouncing along. He had a pair of barbecue tongs, which he used to stuff the snake into the bag. "Trash?"

Some niggling urge hit Wacey, and he shook his head. "No. I need to call TJ. Put it in the garage."

Peter grinned. "No problem, man. I can do that."

"You don't have to seem so gleeful, Peter." Mama looked like she was fixin' to cry.

"Sorry. Sorry, Mama Bene." Peter sobered.

"Go on. I'll mix drinks. A snake. In my house."

Pop looked at him when the rest of them had left. "Call TJ? You think someone put it there?"

"Pop, when was the last time we saw a rattlesnake up here?"

"Been a long, long time. Never in the house."

"No, never in the house, in the closet with the door that had been shut."

"You sure? You've been a little out of it."

"I'm sure. Mama was in here. She would have shut it." She had this weird thing about open doors.

"Well, shit. You call TJ. I'll check to make sure Pete hasn't run off. If he did it…."

"Why would he come to do that? Y'all called him."

"We did. I don't know, son. Come on and sit with us, and I'll have Dee call TJ so no one is the wiser."

"Works for me." He grinned at Pop. "You bashed that rattler like a trooper."

"You softened him up." Pop put an arm around him. "I still got it, though."

"You do that, sir. You got it in spades."

Pop guided him out to the den, half supporting him. The adrenaline thing was getting pretty damned old. Hell, he'd quit competing because of how tired it made him.

"We need to get you back to therapy, son. It was helping."

"I know. I've just been so tired." He felt a little like a five-year-old again, trying not to pout at being chastised.

"You want me to beat up someone?"

He snorted, then started laughing for real. Pop had always, always been able to make him laugh.

Chuckling, Pop eased him into the den and down on the couch.

"What are you two laughing about?" Mama asked. "This is not funny!"

"It was pretty funny." He met Pop's eyes, and they both cracked up again.

"Oh, you two. Los hombres siempre piensan que son divertidos. You're not, okay?"

"Okay, Mamacita. Okay." Pop grabbed her and kissed her, spinning her around. "We were laughing at each other, Mama, not the snake."

"Oh. Well, you're still jerks."

That set Wacey off again, and he hooted, holding his belly.

"Aw, man, did I miss a good joke?" Pete came back in, smiling.

"Maybe two or three of them."

Pete flopped down on the couch next to him. "You know I love a bad joke."

"You love laughing, dork fish." No way Peter did this to him. No. Fucking. Way.

"I do." Peter went serious for a moment. "Did someone just try to kill you, Dub?"

"I think someone's been trying for a little while."

"Shit. Shit. So it started at the rodeo and followed you here?"

"I don't know. I don't know, man. Am I that bad?" Was he that big of an asshole?

"Yes." Pete gave him a laughing look. "The worst."

"Good to know." Dammit. "Bring me a damn drink."

"Here, man." Rusty handed him a Bloody Mary.

"Thank you, sir. How's it going?" Rusty had been the entertainer back when Pop had worked the rodeo, but jokes required a guy to be current, and fat wife jokes were passé, so Rusty had come home to the school.

"Well enough, I guess. Some of these kids don't want to learn nothin'."

"No? Well, you can lead the horse to water."

"That's what they say." Rusty stared at him just long enough to make him twitch before breaking into laughter. "Good thing I have a great sense of humor."

"That you do, buddy." Pop wandered back in, winking at Wacey. "That's all done, son."

"Thanks."

Pete grabbed the remotes. "What are we watching?"

"*Tombstone*."

"Again?"

"Mama has a thing for Wyatt Earp."

"I like Doc Holliday," Pete said. "He's hot."

Yeah, yeah. He agreed. He wasn't going to say so, but he did. Wyatt was nice, especially the Kurt Russell edition, but Doc was broken in the best way….

"Lord." Rusty waved off. "I'm gonna get back to work."

"It's awful late, buddy." Pop didn't argue more than that, though, settling down in his chair.

Rusty snorted. "Never too late to practice."

What Rusty was practicing for, he had no idea, but once the guy left the room, Wacey felt more comfortable.

He just wanted to rest, have a second to breathe.

Mama made popcorn not long into the movie, they all drank their Bloody Marys, and Wacey felt better than he had in forever.

Maybe, just maybe, he'd put on jeans tomorrow.

Chapter Thirteen

TJ frowned at the sky as he drove to the Bene Ranch. The forecast said rain and wind for the next week, and he was a sunshine kind of guy.

Lord knew he needed all the good stuff he could get when his job could show him the worst of the world.

He pulled up to the gate and pushed the button. He'd taken his truck rather than the department car, because Mr. Bene had clearly wanted to keep this on the downlow. So much so that TJ had a cold trail of about fourteen hours on the new incident. He hadn't gotten the message until he stopped by the office on the way to the diner.

Stubborn cowboys. Seriously. Those Benes were closemouthed as hell. Dee had been the one to call it in, Mike said, and he was the one person who hadn't seen dick.

Dammit.

Still, he could totally see Wacey again. He'd fucked up somehow, and it was time for a do-over.

The gate slid open, so he pulled through and headed up to the main house. Dee had said the snake was in the garage.

Pop Bene was sitting on the porch with Wacey, both of them drinking coffee.

He stepped out of the car, then pulled out the bag of sausage-and-egg biscuits from the diner. There was a big box of hash browns as well.

Never let it be said he didn't know the way to a cowboy's heart.

"Morning, gents." He stepped up on the porch. "Breakfast?"

"Well, I'll be. Come on up, Chief." Pop Bene grinned at him, nodded. "I'll have Mama get you a coffee."

"Thank you, sir." TJ settled in next to Wacey. "Hey."

"Hello there. How's it going, man?"

"Not bad. Kids are crazy busy, but that means I have time on my hands." TJ grinned. "You get some sleep?"

"I did. Week's worth. Haven't so much as done shit."

"Good deal." He opened the bag, tickled as hell that Lana had thrown two extra sandwiches in. He had enough for Mama Bene too.

"Yeah. You here about the little surprise in my closet?"

"Dee called it in last night. Late, I guess. When did it actually happen?"

"Between eight and eight thirty."

"Give me the lead up." TJ unwrapped a breakfast sandwich. "Grab you a sammich. They're good."

"Thanks." Wacey grabbed one, then leaned back. "Peter had come over to give me shit, then I got up and got a shower."

"Peter?"

"Peter Nunn. You remember him from high school?"

"Wacey, I have picked him up a half-dozen times over the years for trespassing. I know him."

"Trespassing?" Wacey blinked at him. "What kind?"

"He gets all artsy-fartsy and ends up inspiring himself on Miss Rose's roof or following a herd of deer naked. He's harmless."

"Oh." Wacey chuckled. "I told Pop there was no way Pete did it."

"You don't know that it just didn't slither in on its own…."

Wacey gave him a hard look. "TJ. When was the last time you got a call for a rattler up here?"

He'd opened his mouth to answer when Wacey interrupted. "And I know it's a rattler."

"Okay. So how did it get in your closet?"

"Well, you know, I missed you and couldn't figure out how to get you back out here, so I bought one and hid it in my closet."

"Not funny." TJ grinned, though. He liked the idea that Wacey missed him.

"I don't know. I'm pretty sure the closet was closed before I showered."

"So while you were in the shower."

"Had to be," Pop Bene said, bringing him a coffee before grabbing a sammich.

"Thank you, sir."

"No problem. So, how did they get in?" Pop Bene just looked flummoxed. "All the windows have bars because so many are cracked for the summer."

TJ chewed a moment, pondering. "Who all was in the house?"

"Mama, Pop, Rusty, Peter, me…. I think that's it."

"Okay. Can you check with your mom on that? No rush, but she might know if someone else on staff was here."

"Of course. Sure. She's not coming outside until the snake is gone."

"Oh, no. I'll take her a sandwich." TJ rose, feeling as if he needed to reassure Mama Bene.

He heard Pop and Wacey laughing, but it was his job to make things better, to ease her fears. He took the wrapped sandwich, this one bacon and egg. She deserved bacon.

"Morning, Mrs. Bene. I brought breakfast."

"Good morning, TJ." She came to him, hugged him, and then backed away and patted his cheeks.

"Bacon and egg on biscuit. You okay? I know that had to be scary last night."

"You know I hate those beasts. You'll take it away?"

"I will. I'll have to send it out to the lab. No one has seen any sign of it?" Mama Bene was terrified of snakes. Anyone who saw snakeskin or rattles, garden snakes or burrows had to immediately report it and get Shane, their resident snake wrangler, to handle it.

"No. No, not a sniff."

"Okay. Was there anyone else in the house? Wacey says you, Pop, Pete, and Rusty."

"Right. The girls and grandbabies were at home, none of the cowboys had come up."

"That doesn't leave us a lot."

"The closet door was closed. I went in to see Wacey's sheets. See if I needed to change them. The door was closed. Then, when he came back from his shower, it was open."

"Ah. You're sure?"

"Tomaso. El cucuy. You know."

Right. No boogeymen for Mama Bene. She made sure doors were closed and the area under the bed was covered with a bed skirt.

"Yeah. Was the window open?"

"Yes." She nodded immediately. "For the swamp cooler. Mijo was running hot."

"How about the doors? They locked?"

"At that time of day? No. No reason."

"Shit." That meant any number of people could have slipped the snake in. "Pardon my French. I'll need to look outside. You eat up, and I'll take that carcass to my truck, okay?"

She patted his cheek. "You're a good boy. Come in, after. I'm making tortillas."

"Thanks, Mama." He clapped his hat back on when he stepped outside. He didn't hold much hope for anything outside Wacey's window, and he was right. There was still a dizzying myriad of footprints and scuff marks from the feed incident, since it hadn't rained or blown.

There were bars on the windows, though, so someone would have had to fed the snake through them and managed not to get bit or there had to be someone from inside. There had to be.

If he ruled out Mama Bene and Pop and Wacey, well, that left Rusty and Pete of the guys he knew were in the house.

Huh. Rusty was just an old clown and had been a friend of the family as long as anyone could remember. Hell, he thought there was a good chance Rusty was Wacey's godfather. Pete, though, Pete could be tricky. He thought Pete was pretty harmless, but who knew if he'd been harboring resentment all these years? TJ would have to stop by and see him.

But someone would have noticed Pete in the feed, right? The man wasn't particularly inconspicuous. Dee had been right there that first night in the barn too. Pete had a dirt bike. Someone would have heard that.

Christ, his head hurt.

He just didn't run into a lot of whodunnits out here. He headed back to the front porch, hoping the gents had left him a sandwich or two.

Pop glanced at him curiously.

"Nothing conclusive outside Wacey's window. I'll need to look at the closet, but I need food."

"Good thing you brought some with you, man." Wacey pushed the bag toward him.

"I did! Smart of me, huh?" He grabbed a sandwich, thinking how he said *sammich*, but his kids said *sanguich* like his ex-wife did.

He noticed the cowboys beginning to trickle into the kitchen in twos and threes, each leaving with a bowl of beans and a foil packet of tortillas.

Mama had promised him some of that too. He'd grab some on the way out for the day's work.

"I see you eyeing the beans, son. Grab you some."

"Thanks, Pop. Wacey, can you walk me through to your room a minute?"

"Surely." Wacey hauled himself up and grabbed his crutches.

He wanted to offer to help, but truth was, Wacey needed to get his shit together and do for himself. Get back to physical therapy. Wacey did all right, but was sweating by the time he got to his room. He sat on the bed.

"Okay, so you were in here, what? Sleeping? Watching TV?"

"Before my shower?"

"Yeah." He needed a timeline. He needed to establish when someone might have had a chance to put that snake in. What if it happened earlier and someone just had to slip in and open the closet?

Wacey blushed dark. "I was sleeping. I had been taking some time off. Then Peter showed up with a milkshake."

"Hey, you needed the rest. You keep getting hit. Okay, so sleeping hard?" Wacey used to wake at the slightest noise, but an injury could change a man.

"Sleeping pills. I have a prescription."

"Ah." So someone could have gotten in there anytime during Wacey's nap. "And the closet door was closed when you went to sleep and woke up?"

"I'd been in bed for a bit, but I'm sure it was. There wasn't any reason for it to be open."

TJ grinned. "Your mama is kinda psycho about it." He got it, though. James was absolutely emphatic that all closets be closed before sleep was to be had.

Wacey rolled his eyes, but nodded. "The cucuy. It's a thing. You tell your boys about that one?"

"No. Monica did. And la llorona. And el coco." Monica loved to tease the boys with all the monsters, Anglo and Mexican.

"Lord, Lord. So, you don't think it was Peter, do you?"

"I don't want to. He's not malicious, as far as I can tell, but there's no saying he's not doing drugs or harboring a grudge from years ago."

Wacey gave him an arch look. "Tank, if he was harboring a grudge all these years, it would be against you. You wiped his chance right out."

"What? Chance at what?" He didn't get it.

"It doesn't matter." Wacey rolled his eyes like he was an idiot of the worst kind.

TJ would ponder that later. He walked to the closet, and the irony of the idea wasn't lost on him. He opened the door, peered inside to see if there was a light.

There was a socket, but the bulb was sitting on the floor, unbroken. *Huh. Shit.* He bent to look at it closer, the scent of snake still lingering, along with a relatively significant scattering of sand.

"Hang out here for a minute, huh?" He hustled out without explaining, but he needed gloves and a couple of baggies from his truck. He didn't carry a full kit, and if he was going to have to do heavy-duty forensics, he called in the state police, but TJ knew basic evidence collection like any trained investigator.

When he got back, Wacey was sitting on the floor in the closet door, using the flashlight from his phone. "There's no sand leading in, man."

"Yeah? Has anyone cleaned your room since then? Vacuumed?" He had a feeling the sand was from the bag the snake had been in.

"Nope. Mama won't come back until you've told her there's none left. She doesn't believe Pop."

"I'll double-check. You need help up?" Wacey was kinda blocking off everything.

"I'll just scoot out of the way." Wacey pushed himself backward.

"Like a crab, man." That looked painful, but he didn't say anything else. As soon as Wacey left TJ a clear path, he squatted down and used his flashlight and phone to take pics. Not ideal, and he didn't have any markers in his truck, but he had found some business cards and a Sharpie. He numbered them one and two, then laid them out with the sand and lightbulb.

"If there's a bag in there, pull it out, because I don't think I have any?"

He shone the light all the way to the back of the closet. "You mean like a sports bag? There's a black duffel, size small, shoved all the way in. Still has tags on it."

"No. No, like something you'd carry a snake in."

"I don't see any feed sacks or anything." Didn't people carry snakes in white bags? Or with catch poles or something?

"Bummer. I mean, it would probably be weird if there was a bag in there that said 'killer snake' on it."

"Easier for sure, but weird," TJ agreed. He carefully gloved his hands before pushing sand into a baggie, then collected the lightbulb.

"I didn't do that." On that, Wacey sounded sure. "I couldn't have. I don't have my up-on-tiptoes back."

"No, I bet not." And there was no way pocket cowboy there was gonna reach without tiptoes. Or a stepladder, which would have been pretty obvious.

He grabbed the sports bag, then backed out of the closet. "So this is yours?"

Wacey frowned slightly. "I sure don't remember it. Maybe Mama stored it in there."

TJ peered inside, checking for sand or snakeskin slough. Rattles. Something. "Well, if it's not yours, the tags might lead me somewhere." He glanced up, meeting Wacey's eyes. "You know I never thought you did this. Any of it. I had to be careful and consider every alternative."

"I know." Wacey sighed softly. "I think I'm going to need a hand up off the floor, Tank."

TJ set aside the evidence, including the bag, on Wacey's dresser. Then he moved around to brace Wacey's feet against one of his and grab those raised hands. They danced a moment after he hoisted Wacey up, and then TJ swung Wacey to sit on the bed and flopped down next to him.

"Christ. They haven't changed out your mattress since you were a teenager."

"No shit on that, man." Wacey leaned for a second, chuckling softly. "I have *got* to get out more."

"You so do. If you need someone to take you to therapy, holler. I can usually spare a half hour to drive." He let Wacey soak in his strength, breathing deep and smelling Wacey's shampoo.

"You're busy, man, and we're out here. I appreciate it, though. A lot."

"No problem. I would get to see you some for something not criminal." Why couldn't he just let it go? TJ wanted more with Wacey, and what could have been, haunted.

"I'm not sure that's ever going to happen. I seem to be bad luck."

"I think it's more that someone is out to get you. I notice you never thought it was me."

"You're a white hat, Tank. I've called you a lot of names over the years, but you're not a sneaky little bitch."

"Thanks." He pinched Wacey's hip, keeping it as gentle as he could. TJ didn't want to move too much. He felt like a teenager again, the crazy excitement of Wacey's body against his a feeling that had never faded over the years. Not a bit.

Wacey seemed happy to sit there, rest for a second. No sounds, no fidgeting—just this quiet. Contained. When had he learned that?

TJ let it go, closing his eyes for a moment. Stillness was a total luxury for him.

"Are y'all meditating? Is this some sort of psychic snake-warding thing?" Macey stood in the doorway, grinning wide. "You're awake! I'm so proud."

"Shut up," Wacey muttered, easing away from him.

TJ rolled his eyes. "Still a giant pain in the ass, Macey."

"Nowhere near what Lace is. Your nieces and nephews want to see you, man. Can I bring them after school?"

"Sure." Wacey grinned a little. "I actually feel pretty good."

TJ snorted. "No jumping."

"No one lets me have any fun…," Wacey complained, and Macey snorted.

"Right, Dub. You're abused. Is it true? About the snake? Did you bury it?"

"It's in a cooler in the garage."

"No touching. I need to take it as evidence," TJ warned. He'd meant to get the thing out of the garage for Mama Bene's sake, but had gotten distracted.

"Damn. I was going to show the kiddos. Mama made tortillas. Y'all ought to come out."

"Yeah. In a minute," Wacey said.

"Two shakes," TJ agreed.

"Cool. Lacey is coming by. She heard you were awake. She wants to apologize and make up. She feels awful."

Lord, the Bene girls were a handful, but they were good eggs.

"Good deal. Anyone heard from Kace?"

"Pop's on the phone to him, right now. You want I should have Kace call you?"

"Please. In an hour or so."

"You got it." She flipped them a wave and bounced out of the room.

"Your people are still wonderful and exhausting," TJ said.

"Some things never change. It's quieter on the road. There, it's just Kace and me."

"He excited for the chance to take over for a bit?"

Wacey shrugged. "A little overwhelmed, but rocking it."

TJ nodded, knowing he was borrowing time, but not willing to just up and leave. He wanted—oh, hell, he wanted a kiss.

"I think he's actually enjoying being the boss, believe it or not."

"Are you really bossy?" TJ could see that. Wacey wanted what he wanted when he wanted it.

Wacey shot him a surprised look. "Tank, I'm an out gay man in one of the most dangerous sports on earth. I weigh half of what a bulldogger does, and I come to a few guys' belly buttons. I'm the bossiest son of a bitch on earth, and that includes my family."

"Oh, I dunno. Lacey is… wow."

Wacey twisted his nipple. "Don't you talk about my sister."

"Oh! You were the one wanting to kill her." He grabbed Wacey's hands. "No pinching."

"I can kill her. She's my big sister. You, on the other hand, have to deal with me."

"Dangerous man." He grabbed Wacey in a hug, trying to keep it light. "I'm glad you're feeling better, Wace."

"I am too. I never got to say thank you for lunch the other day." Wacey kissed his cheek, the touch soft and gentle.

A thrill raced through him, and he wondered if Wacey could feel his heart pounding against his ribs. "We'll have to try it again sometime soon. Maybe actually get to eat."

"Shit, maybe I can actually have a beer."

"That sounds good." Not at the local watering hole, though. Too many fights. He didn't need Wacey getting all busted up again. "Maybe… maybe one day you could come over and have one."

"Maybe." Wacey leaned away. "Let's see if I can work on that not-dying thing. Tortillas and beans?"

"Sounds good." He caught Wacey before he could rise, then leaned over to kiss that sweet mouth. Just once. Then he rose so he could hold out a hand. "Come on."

"Thanks." Wacey blinked, then took his hand. "Seriously, Tank. Thanks."

"Anything for you, Wacey Bene." He left it at that, getting Wacey up and moving. He had a snake to clean out and, if not a killer, then a fuckwad to find.

Chapter Fourteen

WACEY limped out of his therapy, wondering why on earth he had been so insistent on driving himself.

Maybe because he'd spent the last ten years on the road and he was chomping at the bit. Maybe because he wanted some freedom. Maybe because he wanted to listen to a little AC/DC on the radio. Loud.

He got to his truck and sat for a minute in the cab, his whole body feeling like a punching bag. *Okay. Breathe. In and out.*

In. Out.

He needed a beer.

Oh. A beer. Nothing big, nothing illegal. Just a beer at somewhere not home.

Maybe he ought to call Tank. Not while he was driving; that might get him killed at this point.

Maybe he'd stop at the Oasis and then call. That might work. If it didn't, at least it was a plan.

He reached up to turn the key, and his phone went off, damned near giving him a heart attack. Wacey grabbed at it, fumbling as he tried to get his sweaty fingers to swipe.

"Hold on! Hold on! Hello?"

When he finally got the stupid thing to his ear, he heard a very familiar warm chuckle. "Did I get you at a bad time?"

"No. No. Hey. Sorry, I was just done with therapy. What's up?"

"Well, the kids decided to go to a pizza party and stay over at their cousin's. Want to come have a beer? I have pizza rolls and ranch dip."

"Are you serious? I'd love to." *Wait. Good idea? Bad idea? Fuck it.* It was his idea. Now he didn't have to ask.

"I am. Come on. You know where my place is? Just off Mesa Road on County Road 50."

"Okay. I'll look for it. Are you off the road?" *Are you sure?*

"Not far off. Maybe a hundred yards. I have one of those ten-acre lots Milton Hernandez sold off."

"Ah. Okay. Okay, right. I remember those."

"Cool. The boys just left, so come on. I'll get the pizza rolls in the oven."

"Do I need to stop and pick anything up?"

"Only if you're picky. I have Corona and Bud Light."

"I'm not picky. See you in a half hour."

"I'm waiting with bated breath." TJ hung up, and Wacey was tempted to stop at Jerry Lee's gas station and buy worms.

What he did, though, was call Peter, because his other option was his sisters, and… ew.

"You're doing what, man?" Peter sounded a thousand miles away.

"Going to TJ's for supper. Like just him and me. Together."

"Jealous! Do you want, like, an escape text?"

"Huh?" *What the hell?*

"You know, I can text you in an hour and you can pretend it's an emergency?"

"Yeah, no. I think we'll manage."

"Do you have rubbers?"

"Shut up, Peter." He wasn't sure he was up to anything that required rubbers.

"Seriously. You need rubbers."

"Peter."

"What? I want to live vicariously. Promise me you'll stop and get rubbers."

"Okay. Dude. Asshole. Goodbye."

He didn't stop. The idea of trying to shift out of the truck made him a tad hysterical. What he did do was get to Tank's house and text his folks. He didn't want them to worry.

Then he stared out the window, wishing he'd been smart enough to bring his crutches. He'd decided he didn't need them three days ago. Ha.

Tank looked out the window, then came out to the truck, wearing a pair of cutoffs and a wifebeater. "You okay, Wacey?"

"Wishing I had my crutches."

"Well, I would offer to carry you, but you'd hit me. You can lean if you want." TJ needed a shave, his evening shadow pretty bristly.

"Yeah. I might." He opened the door, trying to will himself to move.

"Come on, Wace." TJ offered one strong forearm. "I got you."

"Sorry. I just…." Had stiffened up.

"Hey, physio sucks. I got hit by a car two years ago on a traffic stop. Not hard. He was trying to bump me out of the way so he could take off. You remember Rooster Meachum?"

"The guy with the Ronald McDonald hair?"

"Yeah, anyway, he hit the gas, and I went flying. Messed up my shoulder and back for a few months. I did therapy for, oh, twelve weeks? Sucked." TJ got him up, moving, and then it wasn't so damned bad.

"That sucks, honey. Tank. Shit. Sorry." Was that kosher?

"You can call me honey if you want, Wace. Tank might sound weirder to people who didn't know us when." Tank laughed, hauling him into the house. It was a long, ranch-style adobe, and he liked how informal everything was in the front room. There was a huge overstuffed couch, a recliner, and an ottoman instead of a coffee table.

No sharp edges.

"I'm going to ease you down, Wace. You ready?"

"Yeah. Yeah, I'm good." He was doing okay, really. He was loosening up.

"Good deal." Tank put him on the big couch. "So, Corona or Bud?"

"You got limes?"

"A whole bag. I plan on guacamole and chips after pizza rolls and ranch." Tank looked so tickled.

"Then I'll take a Corona, please."

"You got it." Tank moved off to get him a beer, and the smell of pizza rolls began to fill the room.

"I like your house, man." He really did. It was homey as fuck.

"Thanks. The kids keep it crazy, but it would look mostly like this, huh?" Tank brought the beer and a wedge of lime. "What does your place look like?"

"Austin. It's just a furnished apartment."

"Ah. Not like your folks' place at all."

"No. The condo is a… place to sleep."

"You spend a lot of time on the road." TJ shrugged, but Wacey could tell he didn't get it.

"I do. I bet Kace brought in a bunch of cowboys to stay. He always wants to."

"You're the strict one, huh?"

He shrugged, letting the motion turn into a stretch. "I'm the older brother. I'm the boss."

"Sure." TJ plopped down next to him. "Rolls have a few minutes still."

"They smell good." He loved those stupid things.

"They do. The boys hate them. Monica never lets them have junk food, so they say they taste yucky." Tank looked at him, eyes comically wide. "Can you imagine?"

"That's unreasonable. Seriously."

"Right? I mean, at least she lets them have ranch, but Hidden Valley has MSG, so that's right out. She lets them eat at the diner, though. Hello? Lo Melt?" Tank was building up a head of steam, and it was adorable. Just like old times.

"Well, I guess it's healthier…." Wacey lived out of a paper sack most of the time.

"Yeah, but they need to experience McDonald's at least once."

"Whataburger. Dude. Whataburger." Oh, he could have a patty melt. Right now.

"Hell, yes." TJ rubbed his belly, then hopped up when a timer dinged in the kitchen. "Snack!"

For whatever reason, that tickled the shit out of him, and Wacey just started cackling.

Tank peeked out of the kitchen at him. "You laughing at me, bud?"

"I totally am." And Lord knew, he needed a laugh. He needed a bunch of them in a row.

"Well, okay." Tank hooted, the sound so familiar it ached. He brought out a huge bowl of pizza rolls, and a dip thingy with ranch and pizza sauce in it.

"Good Lord, that looks all right." He looked over with a patently shocked expression on his face. "No green chile?"

"You want some? I got a jar in the fridge from Mrs. Gutierrez."

"No. No, I was just giving you shit."

"Oh." Tank grinned. "Asshole."

They munched for several minutes without really talking, and Wacey was shocked at how hungry he was. Therapy really was good for him.

He looked up, and Tank was staring at him, watching him like he was jacking off right there in the front room. "Tank?"

"Huh?" TJ blinked. "Sorry. Sorry, was I drooling?"

"You okay, man?" Because Tank looked sorta dazed, to be honest.

"I forgot how just being around you makes me horny." Boom. Was there truth serum in the pizza rolls? Tank just dropped it out there.

"I appreciate it." Sort of. Did he? It didn't escape him that he was pretty damn broke-dick right now, so he was safe.

"I'm not sure you do." Tank shrugged. "I guess it doesn't much matter. You still like adventure movies?"

"Yeah." He didn't know what to say. God, this wasn't cool. He'd been enjoying TJ, and now this. "You want me to go, man? I can get out of your hair."

"No." Tank turned toward him. "No, I really want to have a beer and shoot the shit. It's just been so long, and, you know, we used to default to fooling around." That grin was wry enough that he had to laugh. "We're not kids anymore, huh?"

"No. Not for a long time. Hell, you're a daddy."

"Daddies have sex, Wace. Well, I hope they do. Been a dry spell." TJ grabbed another pizza roll, then coated it in ranch.

"Yeah. I don't.... Not with people who work with me."

"I bet." Tank chuckled, and then the sound became another big burst of laughter. "We're a pair, huh?"

"We're something, all right. Let's just leave it at that." He shifted and stretched again, searching for a little comfort.

"Here." Tank put the bowl down on the table. "I'm not making a pass. Let me rub some."

"You sure? I'm.... It hurts, man." And he needed someone to make his muscles let go.

"I am. Here, scoot." Tank got him situated before putting those big, warm hands on his shoulders.

He tried not to groan, but he had no choice. It eased him.

"Just let it out, man. I know how good this feels."

"God. Please, Tank. Don't stop?" He moaned deep in his chest.

"Nope. I got a good head of steam now." Tank rubbed deep, better than any massage therapist he'd seen all those times at the hospital.

Wacey let his eyes close, let himself melt and relax and trust in Tank's hands. He knew Tank would never hurt him for all the world, no matter what had passed between them, and when TJ worked down his spine to his lower back, he almost screamed. Those muscles hadn't let go in weeks.

"Honey, Jesus. You.… Come on, lay down, let me at you."

Wacey nodded and moved, stretching out so Tank could touch him.

He lay on his belly on the couch, which was big enough for TJ to kind of straddle just one of his legs, then work on his lower back. Tank pulled up his shirt so the heat penetrated too, those hands amazing.

"You have tattoos?" Tank asked.

"A couple, yeah." He did live in Austin, after all. His ink was all Western—horses, cattle, ropes, barbed wire.

"Nice. I figure once I have to retire I'll get one."

"Yeah? What do you want?"

"A badge star. I'm a lawman all the way." Tank dug in even deeper, making Wacey feel a little like jelly.

"That you are. I'm proud of you."

"Are you?" Tank sounded surprised as hell. "Thank you."

"I am. You've done well." He just did what his family did. They were cowboys.

"Hey, you run a rodeo company. That's a lot of moving parts." Tank's touch gentled when he worked down Wacey's good leg.

"Uh-huh." He was going to turn into goo.

"Are you even listening?" Tank teased.

"No. I'm happy and melted."

"Good. Any other tight spots?"

"No. No." His balls didn't count, right?

"Let me get your shoulders again, huh?" Seemed like Tank didn't want to stop touching him.

"If you're sure." Like he was going to say no.

"I am." Tank moved up against him again, but it wasn't skeezy, even if he could tell Tank was aroused by him.

He sighed and nodded. No touch had felt so good, loosening his muscles and making him feel as if he was floating.

Tank didn't chatter, just put him right to sleep with a lighter, gentler touch.

When he woke up, he recognized the music from *The Mummy*, and guacamole had replaced pizza rolls and ranch.

"Want a cold beer? Yours is kinda flat."

"I'm sorry. Shit, man. I'm sorry."

"Hey, you were out for maybe forty-five. Just long enough for me to run to the bathroom and whack off." Tank's smile was just sly enough to make him wonder if that was true. "I'll get you a beer. Chips and guac right there."

"Thanks. Thank you." He sat up, blinking slow and easy, feeling damn good.

"No problem, man. Sometimes the best thing to do after a massage is sleep. Then pee. The bathroom is the first door on the left." Tank pointed to the hallway.

"Thanks." He stood, forcing himself to focus, take one step after another, his gait easing up as he moved. He would have to schedule regular appointments with Tank if they made him feel like this.

He did his business, then headed out, grinning wide at Tank. "I owe you, man. I haven't felt so right in months."

"Yay. Seriously, I know kinda how you feel, so I'm glad I could help." Tank handed him a cold beer and a new lime.

He drank deep this time, the beer hitting him in the belly. "Oh. Hell yeah."

"Mmm." Tank watched him a long moment, then grabbed a chip and scooped guac.

"Is it good?" He got some too. "Oh man. That rocks."

"Thanks. I make a mean green. Everyone has one or two things, right?"

"Yeah. I can make Frito chili pie in a mini toaster oven."

"See? What else do you do?" Tank munched another chip. He'd always been a grazer.

"I make a mean cinnamon hazelnut latte."

Tank stopped eating to stare at him. "Never let a cowboy make the coffee."

"Shut up." He carried a Keurig in the truck. That way he didn't have to put up with bad hotel coffee.

"I don't make the rules, babe."

"This is true. That's a shame. It would be more fun if you did."

"You think so?" Tank's little smile made Wacey catch his breath. "You seem to think I'm hitting on you because we can't do anything."

"I think you think I'm safe, yeah."

"Don't bet on it, Wace. Not one bit."

"No?" He wanted to believe that, at least a little bit. More than a little bit.

Tank leaned close, one hand planted on the couch next to his legs. He could see every whisker, every separate color in Tank's blue eyes, the little flecks of green and gray always surprising.

"I don't remember you having much stubble, the last time you were this close."

"Late bloomer." TJ rolled his eyes. "You do like to ruin my best moves."

"Are you fixin' to kiss me?"

"As long as you're not gonna get all weird."

"I haven't kissed you in a damn long time."

"I know." Tank moved closer, his lashes dropping a bit to cover his eyes.

He wasn't going to close his eyes. Not a chance. He wasn't ashamed to be doing this, and he wasn't going to hide.

Tank kissed him gently at first, a sweet touch of lips like nothing they'd ever done as teens. He licked a line around Tank's lips, careful not to push, just wanting a taste.

Tank opened up for him, one hand coming up to cup the back of his head. The touch was possibly the hottest thing he'd ever felt.

The kiss went deep and hard suddenly, both of them struggling for control. *Come on, Tank. Show me what you want.*

He got just what he wanted, TJ kissing him until he couldn't breathe. He dragged one hand down that broad chest, his palm open so he could feel Tank's heart race.

They drew back just enough to look at each other, TJ's blue eyes wide open now. Then they dove in again. Not so safe, was he?

This time it was Wacey who closed his eyes, his focus on those drugging kisses. This was real.

Tank moaned, that free hand starting to roam, rubbing the thigh of his good leg, all the way up to the hip.

His body tightened, his whole world focusing down to nothing but TJ, right here, right now.

"God, Wace. You still get to me like no one else." Tank said it against his mouth, hand working up his side.

He didn't answer, because what was he going to say? He reached down and cupped Tank's balls, thumb sliding up and down Tank's shaft as he did. Even through the cloth between them, Wacey knew how much Tank wanted him.

He pushed his fingers into Tank's thin sweats, curling them easily around TJ's cock.

"Fuck! Wacey. Oh, God. Careful."

He looked up, confused as hell. "What, honey? Am I hurting?"

"Only in the best way."

"Aw. Breathe." He took another deep, hard kiss.

Tank gave it right back, kissing and working at the tie of Wacey's workout pants. Wacey noted that Tank's hands weren't shaking, not even trembling a bit.

No, they were rock steady, and Tank was watching him as if the sun was rising behind him.

"You're hard for me." Tank's whisper was a little awed, and didn't that make him feel thirty feet tall?

"I'd have to be dead not to be, Tank."

"I'm glad you're here with me, instead, babe. I love how you feel. Jesus, your touch…."

"Yeah." He knew how good his hand felt. He jacked off every day.

Then Tank got his pants open enough to get a good grip on him, and he understood. Someone else's hand was way better.

TJ had calluses where you wouldn't expect them. He'd seen a lean-to barn out there. Maybe Tank could cowboy up some. God knew, he'd pay to see that.

Right now he wanted to see more of Tank, and he tugged at that loose T-shirt with his free hand.

"What do you want, babe?"

"Skin. Now."

"That means I have to let go of you." TJ did sit back and tug off the T-shirt, leaving him feeling a little cold. "You too, Wace. Please."

"I got scars. Just be aware."

Tank snorted while skinning out of his sweats. "Me too."

He moaned softly at the sight of all that beautiful, fuzzy skin. Oh, that was fine.

Tank helped him out of his shirt and pants, both of them studying the other. "God, Wacey. You grew up, all right."

"Not too much up," he teased.

"Well, you are tiny, but perfect." Tank leaned down to lick along his neck. "And you're stacked to the ceiling. You're like a study in sex."

He lifted his chin and tried to catch his breath. Damn. Tank was making him crazy, and he was finding out he was just healed enough for this.

He managed to grab Tank's cock, measuring it base to tip and found it well worth it. He liked being able to look while he touched, being able to save mental snapshots for when he was back on the road.

"You look hungry?"

"Do I?" Was that a suggestion? Because he knew how to suck. "Bring yourself up here, and I'll show you."

"Seriously?" Tank blinked at him, then moved fast, pushing off the couch to move around and stand, giving him an easy angle.

"Seriously." He closed his eyes and let his cheek slide along Tank's heavy shaft, let himself inhale deep. Dark, hot, and musky, Tank made his mouth water. He stole a kiss down near TJ's balls, then dragged his tongue up along the heavy shaft.

TJ dug a hand into his hair, gentle, but firm. Holding him right there so Tank could push up a little. He chuckled softly, licking the ridge around the tip.

"That's it, babe. That's the spot."

He didn't remember TJ being vocal. He liked it. He liked it a lot. When he sucked in just the head, Tank moaned for him, beginning to rock a little harder, so he moved to nibbling on the leaking slit.

"Killing me, Wace."

"Mmm-hmm." He thought about stroking himself off while he sucked, but really, he wasn't sure he had that much coordination right now.

He'd just focus on the embarrassment of riches before him and save his need for a while. Wacey licked, then sucked the head again, alternating before he really got down to business. He needed to savor this.

He might never get it again.

He stroked Tank's balls, petting them restlessly, gently, and Tank moaned for him, loud and proud. No one was hiding here. Not one bit. The velvety sacs drew up, wrinkling under his touch, and Wacey moaned and leaned in, taking Tank in deep.

He loved this. Loved the taste of TJ's skin, loved how hot it was. The feeling of a man's cock in his mouth was a powerful thing.

Tank cupped the back of his head, a steady series of moans leaving his mouth. He never pushed or hurt, but damn, TJ was eager as hell. Wacey opened up and let Tank in, let himself suck and pull, taste and moan.

"Please." Tank swayed, panting. Those muscled thighs clenched and unclenched.

He had this. He had this down, no problem.

Hot, salty drops began to fall on his tongue. Tank was so ready to burst for him. He went down, swallowing hard, giving TJ the best he had.

That was it. Tank shouted, that hand in his hair tightening until his scalp prickled. Then Tank came for him, hot and wet, a rush of bitter and salt.

He swallowed hard, slapping the shaft over and over with his tongue, making it last. He pushed up under Tank's balls, asking for every drop.

"Jesus. Jesus, babe. Please."

Wacey knew at this point Tank was asking him to stop as much as to go on. Everything got super sensitive, and it could be too much.

He eased up, leaving Tank with a soft kiss to the tip of his cock.

"Damn. Damn, babe. That was—" Tank turned to plonk down next to him, breathing hard. "Thank you."

"Mm-hmm." He leaned a little, breathing.

"So good to me. You always were." Tank began to pet him again, sliding those rough fingers over his neck, then his chest.

His eyelids felt damn heavy, but he watched, wanting to see all he could.

"Stay with me, now, Wace. There's more to come."

"I'm right here, Tank. Right here." And hard as a rock.

"I can tell." Tank kissed him again, tongue tracing his lips, and grabbed his rigid dick in hand, stroking up and down.

That touch wasn't hesitant at all. No, TJ knew what he wanted and knew how to get it.

Wacey watched, staring as Tank touched him. God, that was pretty.

Tank was eating him up, watching his cock like he was the finest thing ever.

His body knew what to do, and he sank deeper into the couch to keep from hurting himself by going too crazy.

"I have you. Just let me love on you."

The words made him smile. How many times had he fantasized about this? Tank had always been all about getting off and getting back to normal. This was a slow exploration that took his breath.

"I know. I know. I was a stupid kid."

"Shut up, Tank. No apologies." None that the man didn't mean. Not now.

"Mmm. Maybe I just need to put something in my mouth." Tank bent and licked along the head of his dick.

"Tank!" His eyes flew open and his breath stopped in his chest. TJ had never—never once—done that for him. With him. To him. What the fuck ever.

"Yum." Tank grinned up at him before sealing those soft lips around him and sucking.

"Oh, sweet Jesus…." He could die now. He sighed softly and sank into the cushions, feeling as if he weighed more than the earth. His body was just… in shock, maybe.

Tank didn't say anything else, just set to touching and licking, then bobbing up and down like he was in a porno.

Okay, he was having a wet dream. Here. Right here on TJ's sofa. Oh. Oh man, that would be a problem. He pinched himself, just to make sure.

Tank popped off his cock. "What are you doing?"

"Making sure this is real and I'm not unconscious, jacking off on your sofa."

"Not a dream." TJ stroked his thighs, then took his cock in hand and went back to slurping, sucking, the sounds insanely erotic.

"Not a dream," he whispered, daring to reach out, stroke Tank's hair.

That mouth worked him, lips and tongue moving in perfect concert with Tank's hand, which he rubbed up and down. Jesus, he didn't want to know where Tank had learned this, because jealousy was a useless fucking emotion, and he was here now, wasn't he? Not some other guy.

No, he hadn't had a blowjob from someone that cared about him in.... *Stop it.*

Ride it out, cowboy. Ride. It. Out.

He sucked in his belly so he could thrust up, but the twinge of pain had him sinking back down. He had to let Tank do the doing.

Tank's hand settled on his belly. "Please, Wacey. Please. Let me do this."

"God yes. As long as you want."

"As long as it takes." TJ moved down, nuzzling the base of his dick, mouthing his balls.

He spread a little bit, that sudden heat unexpected enough to make his jaw clench.

Wacey panted, his body shaking with the effort not to move, wanting to rock and roll. He watched Tank instead, that dark blond head moving, the cords standing out in TJ's neck.

"Fuck, Tank! You're the hottest thing I've ever seen!" The words shot out of him like bullets, firing from him.

He felt Tank's little smile, the hint of teeth.

Wacey imagined he was bucking, like he had done been throwed and the ground was coming, but not yet. Not yet.

Kinda like flying for a very short time.

Tank moved back to really seal those lips around him and suck, and the world sped back up, maybe turned a bit faster than it was supposed to.

His entire body clenched, and he tried to warn Tank he was close, but the sorry son of a bitch scraped one nail along the sensitive skin behind his balls, and he hollered like a fool and shot. Hard.

God love him, Tank swallowed every bit. Like a boss.

Lord love a duck, he tingled all over. Literally. It was like his nerves were on fire.

TJ patted his hip before sitting upright, those amazing abs working under the pelt of fuzz. “That was something else, babe.”

“Uhn.” That counted, right? Sure it did.

Laughing, Tank patted his hip. “Right? That feels so damned good.”

Tank kept touching him, even still. There was no running to cover up, no nerves. Now, they were at Tank’s house and no one was likely to be around until morning, but there was nothing furtive here.

The whole situation felt like an amazing luxury.

“You want another beer?”

“I won’t be able to drive….” He wasn’t sure whether he wanted Tank to take the bait or not.

“So sleep here. No biggie.”

“People might talk.” Wacey had to give Tank a way out.

“So? You should hear what they say about Star. I’ll get the beer.”

“I’ll text home so they don’t worry.”

“There you go.” TJ rolled to his feet, then pulled on his sweats, leaving the T-shirt on the floor.

Wacey sat up, eased his pants on, thanking God he wasn’t having to take and struggle on with his jeans after PT and the best sex he’d ever have. Then he grabbed his phone.

Staying in town. Fine. Love y’all

With Pete? his mom texted back.

With TJ. He waited to see what she had to say about that.

OK. Be good

That was it. Be good. He chuckled. Wacey guessed he had been on his own awhile.

Next he texted Macey. *Spending the night with Tank*

OMG OMFG!!!

Inorite

Lunch 2morrow?

Yeah. Pizza?

God yes. Macey did have a thing for pizza, and she would even buy. They could go to Village Pizza or Wise Pies maybe. *Go. Have fun. Remember EVERYTHING.*

He pocketed his phone with a chuckle, shaking his head.

"You sending compromising pics of me to the press?" TJ teased, returning with a beer.

As much as he hunted those words for underlying worry, he couldn't find any.

"Totally." He chuckled, leaning in as Tank settled right beside him.

"Cool! I haven't had a scandal in my term yet." TJ hugged him close. "Mmm."

"Hell, I'm the most exciting thing to happen to this town in decades."

"You totally are. Well, that and the vulva Star painted on the Flores' horse barn."

"At least it was Star and not Pete…."

"So far as we know. Pete is by far the most talented painter, and it was a lifelike rendition."

"Honey, I'm not sure Peter's ever been close enough to know what one looks like."

"True." Tank chuckled. "Well, it was something. You want to watch some TV?"

"Sure. I spend a shit-ton of time watching movies on the road."

"Yeah? I don't get to watch too many. I had *The Mummy* on earlier, so you can pick."

"No? I have a terabyte hard drive with about a thousand on there."

"Listen to you. Electric Cowboy."

"You ever seen one of us without our phone?" He knew what he needed to know, and he needed to know a lot.

"Nope." TJ shrugged. "I guess I like the idea of unplugging because I'm always on call."

"Sure. I get that." He was always, always on call. No matter what broke on the road—whether it was animal, electronic, mechanical, or cowboy—he got the call.

"Liar." Tank settled him closer. "Tell me about what you do. Like give me a typical day."

"If we're in and set up? I get up first thing, check the arena, talk with all my stock contractors, my managers. I walk the dirt with my lead bullfighter, watch the lights, take some pictures, then I go get my coffee and answer texts. I do a ride around the arena to open the show and hand the big check out every Sunday. Between that, I run my ass off shaking hands with the local bigwigs, making sure none of the cowboys are fixin' to set anything on fire, and talking to the media. At the end, I watch to make sure the cleanup crew is doing their job and I grab a burger and head to the hotel."

"Damn. They keep you busy. That not setting fire thing sounds a damn sight like my job."

"Yeah. Basically I'm the on-site boss. Anything doesn't work, it's my fault. If you make something my fault, then I will come and eat your face."

"Boss cowboy. You sound like your pop a little." Tank kept touching him, stroking his arm.

"Thank you." Wacey couldn't think of a single person he'd rather be like. His pop was a magical man.

"He's a good guy. I forgot how funny he is."

"He's a hoot, especially now that he's relaxing. I think he's going to ask Derek to manage the rodeo school, soon."

"No shit? Just retire outright?" Tank sounded as shocked as Wacey had felt the first time Pop had mentioned it, but really, he had gotten used to the idea. Pop wanted to take Mama to Spain. Portugal. They wanted to go to the Grand Canyon for a week. Why not?

"They want to buy a fancy-assed travel trailer and go."

"I never would have figured it."

"Really?" It made sense to him. Pop'd been a rodeo man. His grandpappy had been a rodeo man. Rodeo men traveled, then they settled down, but the urge for the road could come back on them.

"Yeah. I mean, Pop Bene is the rodeo school."

"True." Still, it was what it was. "I remember when it was Grandpappy's school, when he was in the big house and we were in the adobe that Lacey lives in."

His people had a system and they'd been moving through a handful of Turquoise homes for generations.

"Yeah." Tank leaned on him. "My folks just up and went to Taos."

"Is it a nice place?" Were they really just touching and talking?

"It is. Dad has twenty-ish acres to run horses and weird herd animals, and Mom has a huge studio."

"Rock on. You have horses, huh?" *Tell me about your life, Tank.*

"Yeah. I got a couple of them when the boys came along, because I wanted them to have animals. I mean, I love to ride, and the boys have ponies right now."

"We ought to ride together sometime, huh? Kace has my Dawson. I miss him."

"I would love that. I have a big, rawboned buckskin and a dapple gray that rides like a rocking chair." Tank sounded so proud.

"You'll have to show me in the morning. I'll help you feed."

"You got it."

They sipped beer, and he clicked through Netflix. They finally decided on a movie, but he really wasn't paying attention.

He was with Tank, here, quiet, together.

The closeness made him happy, deep inside, and he could just stay right here as long as possible.

Chapter Fifteen

TJ grinned down at Wacey, who lay in his bed. That was a fine, fine thing. So good.

Now, of course, he had to get Wacey up so he could go to the diner later for breakfast. Wacey had offered to feed, and TJ wanted him to meet the two geldings and the kids' ponies.

He reached for Wace, hands sliding over the warm skin, the ropy scars, loving the feel of Wacey under his hands. TJ actually allowed himself a little fantasy where he did this every morning, where he and Wacey were a thing. A real thing.

He knew better, didn't he?

Wacey stretched. "I like your bed, Tank."

"Do you? I do too. Firm but with that bit of pillow top." It was also huge. He'd bought a new one when he'd gotten his own place. Monica had kept the four-poster they'd had together.

"I meant that you were in it, but that part's good too."

"Oh. I like you in it." He bent down to kiss Wace on the mouth. "Did you mean it about the feeding?"

"You know it. I don't have my boots, but my tennis shoes ought to work."

"They should, yeah. These guys are all pretty well-behaved." TJ helped ease Wacey to a sitting position.

"I've been stepped on before."

"And kicked. And bit." TJ had seen Wacey take a kick right to the chin from a bucking mare.

"And shit on." Wace gave him a wry grin. "When the horses in the pen went up, I knew it was all over."

"Yep." He showed Wacey to the bathroom and set out some clean sweats and a shirt.

He couldn't imagine how scared Wacey must have been, how bad it must have hurt to come back after all these years.

TJ shook his head. He was glad to have this time, but Wacey would move on, go back to work. He had to get used to the idea.

"Okay, Mister Tank. Show me your ponies before you go hold court. I know you're itching to get to town."

"You gonna come have breakfast with me?" He looked Wacey over. The sweats were ridiculously big, but he looked better than he had the night before.

"Would you want me to?"

"I would." The boys wouldn't be there today. They both had activities. He needed to get them into the rodeo pipsqueak thing soon so they could meet Wacey.

"I'd like to. Let me see if I have real clothes in my truck. I wouldn't be seen like this, not with you."

Vain, proud cowboy.

"You got it, babe. Let's feed first, in case we get gross."

They headed out to the pasture, where all four of the horses milled, knowing what was to come. TJ whistled, then cupped his hands around his mouth. "Buck! Cloudy!"

The horses came rushing to the fence, and suddenly TJ tensed. What if Wacey freaked? What if there was no way he could…?

"Well, look at y'all! You're fat and sassy, aren't you?" Wacey was all smiles, and he climbed the fence to see them, the action familiar if a little hitchy.

Cloudy was a little shy, but Strawberry and Keely weren't, and Buck had never met a stranger, and TJ didn't think there was a horse alive that didn't love a Bene.

"They really are gentle. You need to get you a mare to lead the herd, though."

"I thought about that, but I haven't had time to go to auction."

"I'll see what I can round up. Pop and Macey and I are talking about heading to Ruidoso to see what they have down there."

"Yeah? I love the idea of getting a mustang, maybe, but I need to make sure she's gentle enough not to hurt the kids, even if she's not ridable." TJ liked the idea of a rescue, of doing something good and showing his boys what it felt like.

"You know us. We're horse people." Wacey winked, and they both cracked up, because there was a huge divide between the horse property owners who ran stables here in town and the Benes' place.

Vast.

Horsey folks wore helmets to ride and rode English and looked right down their noses at the trashy rodeo folks, their words. He'd had more than one call from folks in those horse properties complaining about drunk cowboys in town making trouble when really it was high school kids playing mailbox baseball.

Then there was the constant refrain of the Benes abusing their critters.

Nonsense.

No one wanted to be a steer in a rodeo, but no one wanted to know what happened to steers regardless.

Hamburger had to come from somewhere.

Plus, with Wacey running the show, there wasn't a horse that wasn't well-shod, well-fed and cared for, bucking or not. TJ had heard tales of Wace tossing guys out on their ears.

Wacey had climbed into the pasture and was giving love, wandering through TJ's tiny herd without the slightest fear.

"Strawberry will nip. I bet you can tell which one she is." He left Wacey with them, heading off to get the feed.

"Yeah, no worries." Wacey paid attention, at least to horses. Seeing Wacey with them made TJ think that maybe the Benes ought to stop keeping Wacey cooped up and send him out to do physical therapy in the pasture.

This was Wacey's element, not some sterile medical office.

They worked together to get everyone fed, Wacey making sure to offer a small amount of sweet feed by hand. "If you ever need me to come feed for you, they'll remember this."

"You think?" TJ teased.

Wacey shook his head. "I know."

"Well, I would appreciate that. Some nights are long, and Monica isn't always able to come out. Junior Watkins feeds for me sometimes, but you know how old he is."

"I do. I'll do it. I don't mind."

"Thanks, babe." He surprised Wacey with a quick kiss. "Okay, let me go put on the business attire. Two shakes."

"I'm gonna look in the truck for jeans."

"Good deal." He hoped he got to watch Wacey change, but TJ needed his uniform shirt and hat. He was lucky he got to wear jeans and boots on the bottom. None of those double-knit pants for him.

The front door opened and shut, then Wacey appeared, a pair of pressed jeans and a button-down wrapped in plastic in hand. "I picked up our cleaning on the way in. I had some in there."

"A cowboy always has at least a shirt hanging in the truck," TJ said. "I put some coffee on before we went out. Want a sip?"

"I do." Wacey stripped out of his borrowed clothes and folded them neatly, letting TJ have another look.

Damn, that was pretty. TJ licked his lips, wishing they had time for a quickie, but small towns had a schedule. He needed to be at the diner soon.

Wacey got his legs in, then looked to him. "Help me stand up? There's nothing to hold on to."

"You got it." TJ moved to help, giving Wacey his arm. He knew soon Wace wouldn't need help, and he was damned proud.

The man's jeans were too loose, too big, and Wacey frowned. "I don't suppose you have an old belt?"

"I do. Hold on." Hell, even if he had to punch more holes in it, he could make it work.

"Thanks. I don't carry spares of those."

"Shit, man. Those huge belt buckles would pull you down right now."

Wacey's laughter filled his house.

He grinned, going to rummage in his closet. "Here, this one is from high school. I was way skinnier then."

"You weren't grown yet." Wacey took the belt, threaded it on, then shrugged into the button-down before tucking himself in and fastening the belt. It was a ritual they all did, but watching Wacey turn himself from the casual man to hot little cowboy made his belly ache a little.

"You need to borrow a hat?"

"I got a hat in my truck. Everyone'll have to excuse the shoes. I'm not steady in my boots yet. Next week."

"It's good to have goals. You good to follow me in, then?" TJ clapped his hat on his head on the way out the back door.

"I am. Hey." One hand stopped him.

"Huh?" TJ jerked to a halt, turning to look at Wacey. "You okay?"

"Yeah." Wacey's eyes were so dark, so serious. "Thank you. For this. I needed it. You."

TJ felt all sorts of emotions well up that he didn't have time for today. So he just nodded and kissed Wacey hard. "You're welcome. Come on, babe."

"I'll be right behind you."

TJ headed out, looking forward to the shockwave he and Wacey were about to cause. Sometimes Turquoise needed to be shaken, not gently stirred.

Chapter Sixteen

"COME on, Pedro. Let's go." Wacey swung up into the saddle, the action easier than it had been yesterday or the day before.

He'd been riding daily for a week now. Mama had damn near swallowed her tongue the first time he'd saddled up, but Pop had his back.

"Let the boy ride. It's the only thing that'll bring him to right. He's a Bene."

Pedro was the next in line of older mounts that just needed some exercise, needed something to do. Wacey swore they knew and they were all waiting their turn. There was a chorus of whinnies and a dozen soft noses poking him every morning when he went to pick his mount for the day.

They headed out, and he stuck his earpiece in, heading past the school as he called his baby brother.

"Yo! Man, you still broke-dick?" Kacey asked.

"Fuck off, Bubba. How you doing? You miss me yet?"

"Some days. The guys are testing me, but I think I'm doing well."

"Sure you are. You're a Bene." They rodeoed. The only one who didn't full-time was Lacey, for God's sake.

"Thanks, Bro. Everything okay on your end?"

He noticed Kacey wasn't asking him when he was coming back.

"I'm out exercising horses. Daddy isn't riding much these days, and Lacey's preggers, so Derek's busy…." And he loved it. He loved working, sure, but this? This was what he was born for, on a bone-deep level.

"Good on you. Means you're feeling better. Send me a selfie."

"I am. You get that shit with the safety men worked out?" They chatted for a while, just business and bullshit, and it was good, real good, hearing Kace sound like he was happy and busy and handling shit.

Maybe he felt a little like a slacker too. Maybe he'd start going out and looking into the school a little more. It would keep him sharp, keep him busy.

Pop wouldn't mind as long as he didn't step on Derek's toes. Derek was in line to take it over, he was pretty sure.

Still, he was bored, and he needed something to do.

"…coming home for a few days in a couple weeks."

"Wait. What? Sorry, Bubba, I missed that."

"We have a few down weeks, so I thought I'd come up for Mama's enchiladas."

"I'd love that. We can put our heads together."

Kace had become more than his baby brother over the last six years. The man was one of the best friends a guy could have.

"Cool. You need me to bring anything from Austin?"

"Grits. Salsa. My good shirts and boots. My buckles and decent Stetson. My goddamn horse."

"Yeah, well, she misses you. So that's one reason I'm coming up. You want H-E-B grits?"

"God, yes. Maybe Mama will learn to make them if I show her. Four boxes?"

"You got it. I'll get you the good salsa too."

"You're a good man. Holler if you need me."

"I will. Thanks, Dub. Love you." Kacey didn't wait for him to reply, just clicked off.

"Love you too, you crazy shit."

He chuckled and hung up, shaking his head. He had long passed the school and was out in the scrub, heading up toward the mountains.

The view still stunned him, and it was one of the things he'd missed the most in Texas. The mountains called him, just like they did any kid from central New Mexico. They were sunk deep into him, like the coyotes and the dust.

A puff of dust kicked up from the dirt close to him, then he heard a ping as something smacked into one of the boulders. *What the fuck?*

He frowned and leaned down across Pablo's withers to look when a line of fire skittered across his back.

He didn't even bother to think, he spurred the horse and took off, keeping himself long and hidden along Pablo's length. "Go. Go, boy. Run!"

Pablo took off like his ass was on fire because he did like to run, even for an older gent. He let Pablo have his head, just set on outrunning whoever it was.

Whoever was shooting at him, for fuck's sake.

He heard the next shots—three in rapid succession—and on the last Pablo screamed, and the saddle began to jitter. *Fuck. Fuck.* He looked for the safest place to get off. They weren't hunting Pablo; they were hunting him.

So the motherfuckers could find him.

He drove Pablo into a wee arroyo cut into the desert, and he used the sage to grab on and let it yank him off. Pablo kept running, driven by pure panic.

Wacey reckoned that was okay, because he was winded and jostled, and he hoped like hell they followed Pablo for a few seconds because he hurt so bad he couldn't move for a couple three long breaths.

He crawled into the lee of the rocks and sage, panting to get his breath before he could even try to get his legs under him. Unarmed, unhorsed, he was pretty well fucked, but Pablo was safer.

His best bet was to get his ass out of the arroyo, ASAP, otherwise he was a sitting duck. A limping duck. A limping quail? Oh, he liked that.

Wacey pulled his belt out of his jeans and his knife out of the sheath, and used them both to help his ass scale the wall and stay under cover of the sage as best he could.

Dizziness made his head spin, and he grunted, trying to keep it together. Pablo was long gone, but the gunshots seemed to be too. *Okay.*

First thing, canteen. Check. Phone. No service, but 90 percent battery, so he'd walk along the arroyo, keeping the mountains to his left. Eventually he'd hit road.

Where there was road, there was traffic and cell towers. Thank God it wasn't too hot yet. The way the sun was beating down, he'd be sweating buckets in no time.

One foot in front of the other. Leastways he wasn't lost in West Texas. Here he had his mountains.

Chapter Seventeen

TJ headed out to the Bene Ranch, a stack of lab results and other forms on the passenger seat. He hummed along with Jason Aldean, a smile on his face and the wind in his hair. He loved old-school two by fifty air-conditioning on a day like today.

Someone was walking down the road, arm waving hard, right about the time that his phone rang.

TJ squinted, hitting the Answer button on his steering wheel. His phone was synced with his truck.

"Tank? Someone shot at me. I'm walking. I just got a signal. There's a truck coming with lights. Tell me it's you."

"Yeah. Yeah, it's me. Shit. Hold on." He slowed, because he didn't want to blow past Wacey. "Are you hit?"

"I'm not sure. Been walking for a little over an hour."

"Fuck." He hoped Wacey knew where he'd started out walking. TJ would want to have a look. "Okay, hop in." He clicked off his phone before pulling off the main road.

Wacey was covered in dirt and dust, and when he tried to ease himself into the truck, the back of his shirt was stained with blood.

"Shit, Wace, you're bleeding." They weren't far from the house. "How far out were you?"

"Thought something grazed me. I went out past the school and toward the mountain. I was talking to Kace, so I wandered a while, and then we ran some after the first shots."

"We?" He helped Wacey stumble around into the seat, then pulled back on the road toward the ranch.

"Me and Pablo. I'm afraid he got hit, but I sent him running. I'm betting he headed for the barn."

"I hope so. I'm gonna have to call Mike out. Can you remember the mile marker?"

"I just now got out on the road. You passed where I came out already."

"Okay. Call your folks and get them ready to clean you up. Warn them too, just in case someone followed Pablo home. I'll call the station."

"Okay." Wacey sighed softly, grinned over. "Do I have to?"

"You do. They need to know, Wace." TJ keyed up his phone again, calling in for dispatch.

He heard Wacey on the phone, talking fast. "Is Mama there? Good. I need a little first aid. Shot. I'm fine. Pablo took off."

"What's up, Chief?"

"I need Mike out on State Highway 313. Right by the Fernandez Arroyo. There was a shooting attempt about an hour ago. Wacey Bene was on horseback. He's been grazed and his horse was hit, he thinks."

"Well, shit. You sure?"

"He's bleeding all over my truck right now." He turned off on the Bene Ranch road, knowing the gate was coming up soon.

"Open the gate, Pop."

"You need EMS? I can call one in."

"No. I'm okay." Wacey grimaced. "Might need an emergency vet for Pablo. Hold up. What, Pop?" A second later, Wacey told him. "Martin says he came in about ten minutes ago with no rider. He was heading to the four-wheelers to find me."

The gate opened, and TJ headed toward the ranch house, eager to get Wacey looked at and examine the horse.

"You can drop me off here. I need to check Pablo and my feet…."

"Fuck that shit, babe. Come on. Inside." TJ was not going to be sent off while the Bene tribe circled the wagons. He wanted to see what some asshole had done to his lover.

His lover.

Huh.

Did one night make Wacey his lover? He sure seemed to think so, and TJ wasn't one to second-guess himself too much.

He parked at the main house. "Do you need help, babe?"

"Are you going to think I suck if I admit I'm scared to land on my feet?"

"No. I think you walked a long way in your boots when you haven't been up and around too long. I bet you got blisters."

"I bet. Okay. Let's get in before anyone sees me."

"Yeah, that's gonna happen." He ducked around and eased Wacey down out of the truck, not really letting his feet touch too hard. He held up a lot of Wacey's weight and ran for it.

God, he had so many questions. Pop Bene was there, scooting them in, Derek and Tim waiting in the kitchen.

"Where are the girls and Mama?"

"Spa day in Santa Fe, you lucky bastard," Derek said. "Strip off your shirt."

"Stop." TJ held up a hand. "Sit. Let me get gloves and bags. I'm gonna need your clothes."

"My clothes? Why?"

"Because they establish where you were, they give me information about the shooter, and they prove you were hit." He said it over his shoulder as he ran back to his truck.

"Chief! Chief? Everything okay over to the house?" The old clown, Rusty Something, came wandering over. "Dub get throwed again?"

"He's fine, bud. Just fine." He smiled brightly before pelting back to the house.

He swore he heard someone laughing, but he didn't have time to stop and search anyone out. He needed to get in there before everyone shed, breathed, or spit on Wacey.

The guys had pulled out a basin of water and washcloths, but hadn't started dragging off Wacey's clothes.

"Thanks for waiting." After he set down his kit, TJ drew on gloves so he could help ease off Wacey's shirt.

The blow was a graze, slicing down along the left side of Wacey's back.

"That's not too bad." He snapped a couple of pictures with his phone. "Let's get you cleaned up."

"Looks like a .223, the way it tumbled along the skin," Pop said. "Did you see anything?"

"No, sir. Didn't hear the shots at first either. Hardly at all."

"Did you hear a shot or feel it first?" TJ asked.

"I saw it. One hit the dust. One hit a rock."

"Then you?"

"Yeah. I was leaning to check Pablo. The shot grazed my back, and I took off. I didn't go back toward the house, because that was the direction of the shots. I think one hit the horse, I don't know. I went down in the arroyo and bailed off. They followed Pablo, I guess."

"How did you end up on the ground? Did Pablo buck?"

"No. No, the cinch came loose and the saddle slipped around. He was safer without me on him."

"Huh. Okay, I'm good. I'll want your jeans too, but I want to go talk to Dee real quick."

"I need to take his boots off." Pop Bene's voice was low, serious. "Do you want them saved for you?"

"Please. I won't send them to the state lab, but I'll need to process them." TJ knew he was doing way more than protocol demanded, but at this point, it was clear. Someone was gunning for Wacey, and they were escalating.

"Okay."

TJ was heading out the door when he heard, "This is going to hurt like a motherfucker, son. Bear down."

God. He winced. Wacey probably had blisters up to his ankles. Was he ever gonna catch a break?

He headed to the barns, the line of buildings like train cars on a track, separating the Benes' from the rodeo school. He had to go to the quarantine barn to find Dee, who was working on Pablo, the poor gelding still shaking and blowing.

"Hola, Dee. How is he?"

"Fine. Bullet got stuck in the cinch strap. He's scared and tired, but no holes."

"Good deal. Where's that bullet?"

"In the strap." Dee gestured to the saddle, which sat over the top of a stall door looking worse for wear. Must have been a lot of banging and sagebrush. "Is a .223."

"Yeah?" Dee had shot his share of rabid animals and cans. He ought to know. "Pop Bene called it."

"Is the one we all carry." The old cowboy shrugged, stroking Pablo's flank.

"Yeah." Yeah, in fact TJ had a .22 rifle in his truck. Still, even as beat-up as this round was, maybe it would give them something. TJ was sick of this jackwagon being one step ahead of him.

"Is Dub okay?" The old man looked worried, but not guilty. Right?

"He'll be okay. He's tired and sore." He hoped. Jesus, what a mess.

"If he needs me, tell him to call, huh? Shit marthy, who's doing this, Chief? Dub is a good hombre."

"I don't know, Dee."

Martin came wandering in, shaking his head. "Mira, this shit needs to cease. It ain't right. You find this bastardo."

Yeah, he was on it. "You have any ideas? Men that are mad at him?"

Martin shrugged. "There's lots, sure. Dub sends folks back down when El Jefe wouldn't."

"Sends them back down?" TJ was as familiar with rodeo as anyone in these parts, but he wasn't a cowboy, really.

"To the school. Like Helio Gonzales six months ago. He was riding safety, but he was missing two of three pull offs, verdad?"

Dee nodded. "You don't do your job, you don't get to stay on the payroll."

"Ah. So the staff, not the riders."

"Sí. Sí. El Jefe, he says men will learn. Dub, no. Dub is… severo? Duro? You know this? Dee?"

"Stern." He thought that was what Martin meant. Wacey was a hard taskmaster. TJ bet he had to be, taking over for Pop Bene. Lot of boot to fill.

Martin nodded. "You must be, to be young and boss."

"I can hold my own, Martin." He chuckled. "You know where Helios is?" He collected the round, then snapped a few more pics of the saddle.

Dee grunted. "Working with the bronc riders today, but he'll break for lunch soon. You want me to send him on up to you?"

"Sure. I'll meet him outside, though, okay?"

"You have a phone number?"

Did he have a phone number? Christ.

TJ tugged out his phone. "What's yours, and I can text you?"

Dee rattled it off, and he put it in. "Got it. Thank you, sir."

"No problemo, TJ." Dee lifted a hand and went back to doctoring, which he guessed meant he was dismissed.

He took the bullet back to his truck, then the need to see Wacey overrode the rest, so he jogged back to the house.

Wacey was sitting there in the front room, his feet raw and tore to hell, just resting on a towel on the floor.

"Are they getting you a soak?" TJ asked. He hated that Wacey was hurting. Again.

"Eh. They're just blisters. I just need some socks. No big."

"You need to make sure they're clean, Wace." He squatted down, peering at Wacey's feet. Christ. Mama Bene was gonna lose her shit. "Do you need stitches on your back, you think?"

"Nope. And we're not telling Mama about any of this either."

"No? I won't have to, babe. Pop is not gonna take a chance on getting her dainty foot up his ass."

"Christ. Can you slap a bandage on it?"

"I can. Let me get that water and more towels." He'd clean up the feet and the back. Everyone else seemed to have disappeared, damn it.

He found them in the kitchen, Pop's face red as a beet.

"I want you two out there gathering up every son of a bitch that so much as looks guilty and bring them to me, one at a time. This is still my place, and that is my son! I will bury the bastard up to the neck in the desert and let the coyotes eat him."

"Now, Pop. I need some more hot water and towels. What I need from you folks is a list of people Wacey has fired or sent down in the last six months. I'll start with Helios."

"Helios? Did he say something about this?" If Pop wasn't careful, the man was going to stroke out.

"No, Pop. Dee and Martin told me he'd been sent down. I think he's been with the bucking horses all morning, but I have to start somewhere."

Derek sighed. "There's a solid handful. Dub has a three-strike policy, and he's damn firm about it."

"Yeah." Pop grinned hugely, a proud peacock.

"Makes for enemies, though," TJ pointed out. "I'm gonna go finish fixing him up."

Pop nodded, the smile faded. "I just got so mad, and I didn't want to take it out on him."

"I'm fine, Pop. Just a little blistered. Ain't the first time. So y'all are thinking this is someone I sent down? Cowards. They want to shoot me, they know where I live." Wacey had a pair of white socks on, the damn blisters leaking through. "Who wants a beer? I fucking deserve a beer."

Stubborn cowboy.

"Will you sit, you idiot?" TJ demanded. "You're gonna get infections. Derek, where is the antibiotic ointment?"

"Right here. I got it and bandages and shit. I think you should soak them, Dub. You hurt your feet, and then you walk funny, and then you hurt all the things."

"Says the man that broke his pelvis," Tim muttered. "I have to go spell my sister. She has all the kids at my spread, and she has to go to work."

"Okay, man. See you later." Wacey lifted a hand.

"I'll walk you out." Pop gave Wacey a look. "Let TJ doctor you, or I'll call Doc Lopez."

"Not Lopez. He's mean."

"Well, be good, then." Pop walked out with Tim, and Derek left to get the ointment.

"Pablo is fine, by the way." TJ pushed Wacey into a chair before grabbing him a Bud from the fridge.

"I know. I texted Dee. Thanks."

"No problem… .22 round was in the cinch."

"Thank God for that. So, I think I have to go out and just stand in the pasture and tell whoever wants to have a duel better come on."

"After your feet heal." TJ sat cross-legged on the floor with the cloths and water and towels. Derek came back in with the ointment, and TJ set to treating those poor feet. He eased off the socks, shaking his head. "I'll need more socks, Derek. Please."

"On it. Then I'm gonna start rounding up assholes and seeing if they smell like gunpowder." Derek stopped. "Dub? Were they on horseback like you?"

"Maybe. I didn't hear anything, but I was on the phone with Kace for a goodly amount. You could have brought a four-wheeler if you were trying to…." Those dark eyes went all thunder and lightning.

"What? What are you thinking, Wacey?"

"The shots came from up, at least at first, but how did they move so fast? They were up and to the right, then it was lower, to my left…."

"You think there's more than one?" Shit. Oh, that would suck. Partners in crime were always so much more unpredictable.

"You always head the same way, Dub? On your ride?"

"Basically, yeah. I know the way, and I was seeing how each horse coped. There are a couple that need more exercise…. Today I started out around the school before I veered for the mountains."

"So they weren't trying to shoot you. You are an easy target. They were trying to unmount you." Derek would make one hell of a cop.

TJ nodded slowly. He rubbed ointment into Wacey's feet. "What the hell is the end game here?"

Pop looked at Wacey, and Wacey stared back, the two men different as anything, but just alike at the same time.

"Is this a standoff, guys?" He glanced at Derek, who shrugged.

"Don't ask me," Derek said. "I mean, the only family member I can see wanting Wacey out of the way, even temporarily, is Kacey. And he's in Austin."

"They don't want me dead."

Pop shook his head. "They want you broke, Dub. They want you broke and hurtin'."

"But why?" TJ pondered that as he crawled up Wacey to get off the floor. "Let me wash my hands and I'll do your back."

"Had to be someone you did bad by, Dub," Derek said. "Who'd you fuck?"

"Not a one. I swear to God. Not a one. I didn't play favorites. You call Kace and ask him."

TJ washed up, chewing his lip all the while. "Helios? Why did you send him down?" He knew what Martin had said, but he wanted to hear it from Wace.

"He wasn't pulling worth a shit. He missed two out of three, three events in a row. I don't know if he was drunk, lazy, hurt, what, but he wouldn't say, and I couldn't keep him. He's still pulling a salary, and Derek's watching him now."

"He's doing great. I think being on the road away from his new wife was just too hard." Derek said it matter-of-factly, and TJ trusted his judgment.

"Who else? Since right before you got trampled?"

"I fired a guy named Will Bowers. I caught him beating up his girlfriend, and I won't have that. Before that I sent Little Jim out because he wasn't going to heal that wrist otherwise."

"Little Jim is too fucking old to be on the circuit, son. I told you that. Him and Rusty, I swear to God, those two held on like ticks."

TJ stared at Pop. "Well, now, maybe I ought to talk to the two of them."

"Sure. I mean, Little Jim is living in Chama now. His grandbaby has him wrapped around his finger, but Rusty's teaching and performing at the junior rodeos."

"Chama." Well, that was a tough one for getting down to shoot at Wacey, but Rusty was right there. "Shit, what time is it?"

"Uh… damn near two I guess?"

"Crap." He'd meant to just drop off the papers and go. "I have to go get the boys. Miz Calleigh at the daycare is taking a long weekend."

"Take Wacey with you. I'm going to speak firmly with Helios."

"Pop!"

"What?"

"That's a good idea, Wacey. Aside from the incident on the road, everything has happened here at the ranch or school. I can keep you out of harm's way."

"I'm not a victim! I can arm myself."

"Son, Lacey is pregnant. Mama is here. I don't want either one of them to get hurt. Hell, I told Tim to make sure Macey and her brood stayed home for now."

TJ touched Wacey's shoulder. "I don't mind at all."

"This is ridiculous." Wacey stood up, fighting his wince, that wound on his back ugly. "You could just say you want me to meet your kids, Tank."

TJ's cheeks heated. "Well, I do. I mean, they need to."

Pop looked back and forth between them, a grin forming. "You gonna bring them to rodeo school this year, TJ?"

He was gonna go up in flames if he blushed hotter. "I signed them up, yeah."

"Good. Good. That works for me. I will meet them too. You want me to pack a bag for you, son?"

"No. I got it."

"I'll be right back." TJ stepped out on the porch and tugged out his phone to call Mike, his second-in-command. Well, there were only three of them.

"Yo, boss. You had one on a four-wheeler, one on foot. The one on foot came from the road. I assume he drove in."

"Shit." Maybe it was Helios and the clown. Why would the other guy come down from Chama just to cause trouble? "Okay, I need you to come out to the ranch once you're done there and talk to Pop Bene. He has two employees I want you to interview."

"Sure, boss. You need to pick up the boys, don't forget."

"I'm on my way." TJ hung up with Mike and called Calleigh, his boys' daycare mom.

"Hey, Teej. Where are you?"

"Had a call. I'll be there in twenty."

"Good deal. I'll have them ready."

"Thanks, lady." He hated being late for them, and Monica was on a double, so this was his responsibility.

"I got it, no problem."

"See you soon." By the time he hung up with her, Wacey was back with him, carrying a wee bag.

"Okay. Ready," Wacey said.

"Come on, then." He took the bag, even when Wacey glared. They headed for the truck, Wacey moving careful. "I can't wait for you to meet my boys."

"I wish it was under better circumstances."

"Sure. I mean, of course." Was he a bad person for kinda forgetting that for a moment? TJ was excited.

"You'd let me meet them anyway?" Wacey climbed up into the cab.

"I would. I really have signed them up for the school."

"Huh." Wacey shot him a look, and TJ thought it was pleased.

He'd take it.

He climbed in the truck, and thank God no one shot at them. TJ got them headed out, mentally changing his plan for supper. "How do you feel about turkey meatballs?"

"I'm all over them. Me and Kace eat a lot of them."

"Cool. I have some, and the boys love them with spaghetti and sauce." Boom. Grilled cheese crisis averted. Wacey hated grilled cheese. Childhood trauma. TJ had always teased him about it back in the day.

His phone dinged, and he handed it to Wacey. "If that's Monica, tell her I'm on my way to get them and C knows."

"Okay." Wacey texted with admirable speed. "Does she have radar?"

"No, she knows my job." TJ chuckled. "So she always reminds me. Always."

"Ah. I get that. That's what I do a lot on the road. Babysitting."

"Yeah. She's exceptional at it. We meet once a week, and I pretend to pay attention while she shows me her planner."

"Pop has one of those. I'm all digital."

"Me too. Well, and I have an assistant at work." Did that count as cheating?

"I have a baby brother."

"True. How's he doing?" Wacey had said he was talking to Kacey when he got shot at.

"Good. I think he likes me being gone."

"You think so? Likes taking the reins?"

"I do. He's gonna hate when I have to go back to work."

"He'll live." TJ wasn't sure he would. Oh, he would survive, but watching Wacey walk away again might just be too much for him.

"Yeah." Wacey handed him his phone back, fingers sliding alongside his.

"Careful. I don't want to run off the road," TJ teased. Not that he didn't mean it. Wacey's touch meant a lot to him. Way more than just memories of the bad old days.

"No. I've had enough of that kind of excitement, and you have to pick up your boys."

"Exactly." He wasn't speeding. Not really. Better to speed now than later with the kids in the car. God, they were both gonna be so fascinated with Wacey. He hoped Wace was good with kids.

He hoped Wacey liked kids. “You ever spent any time with kids, honey?”

Wacey looked at him, face a study in shock. “Tank? I run a rodeo company. You know what cowboys do when they aren’t riding? They make babies. I have eight nieces and nephews and one more on the way. I am the godfather to twenty-eight kids. Twenty-eight. If a meteor hits the motherfucking rodeo? I have a shitload of babies to raise.”

He hooted. “Okay, okay. I just never thought of it like that. That’s good. Real good.”

“I was actually there in the room when Sara McAllen’s baby came. She shot Victoria out like she was peeling a grape.”

“Lord. I was there for Thomas and James both. Monica cussed me a lot.” TJ remembered the whole queasy first time, and how easy James had seemed after. He had to smile; his kids made him happy.

“I imagine so. It was your fault, after all.”

“It so was.” TJ shook his head. “I wouldn’t trade them for anything, but I wish I’d done better by Monica. I mean, I tried. Hard.”

Wacey stayed quiet for a long minute, then simply said, “I’m sorry, man.”

“Yeah? What for?” He kinda blinked over at Wace. None of TJ’s mistakes were his fault.

“You, I guess. I’m sorry you were unhappy.”

“Thanks.” TJ reached over with one hand to pat Wacey’s leg. “Lying is never the way to go, right?”

“No. No, I’m pretty sure it’s not.”

“I’m okay with it now. I mean, Monica and I worked it out.” Was he confessing? It felt like it. Weird.

"How does she feel about me being back in town?" Wacey grinned over at him. "And remember, lying is never the way to go."

"Well, she's pretty pragmatic, although she did make a good argument for you doing this to yourself. So maybe a little worried." TJ chuckled, thinking how not worried Monica was at all. She would want to have lunch with Wacey soon and compare notes.

"I don't think I could shoot myself in the back…."

"No, I discounted that pretty fast. I had to look at it, though. You get that, right?" He wanted Wacey to know he'd never given that theory any real credit.

"I do. I don't want to sleep with someone that thinks I would hurt my family, though."

"I know." TJ understood that. He did. "How's Lacey? Did her dog recover?"

"Yeah. Totally. Lacey came over and sucked ass for a bit; then we were okay. She's hormonal and lost her shit."

"Lord help you. Well, Derek takes the brunt of that, I bet." He pulled up at Calleigh's, parking in front of the little Rainbow Wee Ones sign. She and her wife had opened their place up a few years ago, and TJ adored them both. "Be right back."

He ran in, his boys waiting in the tiny lobby.

"Daddy! You're late!" Tommy was just a stickler for time. He came running down the steps to fling himself at TJ just as he stepped into the little gate.

"I called Miss Calleigh, you know."

"Uh-huh. We missed you, though."

"Daddy?" James tugged his sleeve. "Somebody's in your truck."

"Yep. Come on and sit in your seats so I can introduce you." He hugged Thomas before lifting James into his arms.

"I played with Elijah today, and he didn't bite me." James sounded so pleased.

"Did he bite anyone else?" TJ asked. He swung James into the back seat, his car seat the same size as Thomas's now. Lord knew, TJ got they helped, those seats, but he couldn't wait for the boys not to need them.

"He bited me yesterday." James held up a bandaged finger. "Hello, sir! I'm James Cook!"

"Hello, James Cook," Wacey said. "I'm Wacey Bene."

"Bene?" Thomas climbed into his seat, eyes wide. "Like the rodeo school? Daddy says we get to go ride bulls."

"Like the rodeo school. You'll get to ride the barrel and the mechanical bull first. Then maybe a steer."

"I won a trophy at mutton bustin' at the fair," James announced.

"Did you? That's cool. I have one at my house from when I was your age." Wacey turned to look at Tommy. "And I bet you are Thomas Cook."

"Yessir. We all got trophies." Tommy could be a little mean to his brother when he was trying to impress adults.

"But what did James do?" TJ prompted.

"He stayed on the longest and didn't cry none when he got bucked off."

"And you were so proud you gave him your trophy too, didn't you?"

"That's what big brothers do," Wacey said very seriously.

"You have a little brother?"

"I do. He's a rodeo cowboy like me."

"What event does he do?" Thomas knew events and stats and all. He read everything, researched all things.

"He's a roper. Team roping, tie-down. But his job is chute boss. Right now he runs the whole company for me."

"Wow!" Tommy bounced. "That's so cool."

"Are you hurted?" James asked. "That's why cowboys come home, right?"

"I am, yeah. I got pretty broke up."

"I'm sorry to hear that, sir." Thomas was a little more restrained than James.

"Wacey is coming to spend the night tonight, guys. We're gonna have spaghetti and meatballs."

"Pasghettis!" both boys crowed in unison, and Wacey just cracked up.

"You're now their hero." Once he was sure the boys were all hooked in, he headed home. He let Wacey take the conversation, with Thomas peppering Wace with questions, and Jamie telling Wacey his every accomplishment.

He kept peeking at Wacey, but the man didn't look exasperated or frustrated. No, Wace was paying attention, laughing, talking to them, which given how much Wacey had to be hurting right now? TJ was going to just fall in love.

More in love. Because he wasn't one to kid himself these days.

They arrived at the house a few minutes later, and he helped James out of his seat. "You guys need to go see Strawberry and Keely. They're lonely for you."

"'Kay, Daddy!" The boys ran up to the fence, hollering for their ponies.

He grinned at Wacey. "I make them spend time. At their mom's, they have a dog; here they have ponies."

"Why don't you have a dog?"

"I did. Not long after I moved in. He got hit by a car a few weeks later because he kept escaping the fence, and I knew it wasn't fair to keep a dog when I was never home."

"Oh man. I hear you. I want a dog. I may get me one."

"Yeah? Someone to protect your truck?" TJ missed having dogs around. He went to Monica's a few times a month just to play with her pit mix, Doogie.

"Just a dog."

"Cool. Come on in and take a load off, babe."

"Are the boys okay out here alone?"

"Yeah. I'll keep an eye on them through the kitchen window. Thomas, watch your brother, bud!"

"I will, Daddy! Can we come get some baby carrots for them?"

"Yes, you can if both of you come."

"Come on, James! We'll get them to come faster with carrots!"

James climbed down off the fence, and both boys pelted back toward the house.

Wacey chuckled. "Lord. James looks just like you. Thomas has some of you."

"Tommy looks a lot like his momma, for sure." He listened to the boys bickering over who had the best carrot. "Come sit down, put those feet up."

"Thanks." Wacey gave him a broad wink. "They like apples too."

"Boys or horses?"

"Both."

"Did you hear that, guys? Want me to cut us up an apple?"

"Apples? Daddy, can the Bean-Man have some too?"

"We all can. The ponies have to split one. Too much can make them sick. But you can give them that and carrots while I make us apples and peanut butter." It was too early for supper.

"Do you need help, man?"

"I need you to sit down and relax."

Wacey finally sat, then pulled out another chair to prop up his feet.

He cut up half an apple, the boys rushing outside. God, they made him happy. "You want peanut butter too? Or you want me to get you some Doritos?" He still loved Doritos.

"Peanut butter is fine. I don't see your ex giving them Doritos."

"No, but I have them." He winked, then cut up a few more apples with his apple cutter, a gift from his mom. He'd laughed at her, but he used it all the time.

The avocado cutter and scooper thing not so much.

"Maybe we'll share them for a late-night snack."

Right. He was looking at Wacey. That man was going to crash and burn. Still, he liked the idea of having a late-night foray into snacks with a lover. In his house. In his bed. Wacey. He was gonna short out. "I'm all over that, Mr. Bene."

"Good deal. Mmm. That apple smells good. I think I missed lunch."

"I think you missed most of the day."

"Shut up." Wacey laughed, then shook his head. "I don't suppose I can get an aspirin from you?"

"You bet. I got aspirin, Tylenol, and Aleve."

"One of each?"

"Yeah, no. Aleve. It works longer." TJ grabbed the pills out of the cabinet above the coffee maker. The boys liked to rummage in the medicine cabinets when they thought he wasn't looking, standing on their little bench in front of the sink.

All medications stayed in here, out of reach.

He handed over the pill, along with a glass of water. "Here, babe. This will help."

"Thanks, Tank. I appreciate it."

"No problem. We got to figure this shit out, Wace, or someone's gonna kill your ass."

"Yeah. It's becoming kind of a thing."

"Daddy! Daddy, they ate the apples all gone." The boys came running in.

"The carrots too?" He grabbed Jamie in a hug and swung him around.

"The carrots and the apples." Tommy crawled up on a stool. "Can I have an apple, Mr. Bean-Man?"

"Sure. That's what your daddy cut them up for."

"Thank you."

"You bet." Wacey served up apples and peanut butter, and Jamie wiggled so he could get down to go get his.

He liked that—the sight of Wacey and his boys sitting in the kitchen. Hell, Jamie held up his arms for Wacey to lift him to the stool beside Wacey, and TJ's heart damn near melted.

Wacey was easy with the boys—listening to them jabber on and on, no stress on his face. Heck, when Jamie left his stool and insisted on climbing into Wacey's lap to show him something, Wacey just put an arm round him and listened as if Jamie's thing was the most important thing on earth.

He needed to move them to a softer surface, though. Wacey wasn't showing that he was hurting, but TJ knew he was.

"You guys want to come sit on the couch now you've had your snack? Dinner won't be for a bit yet." TJ knew Thomas had some reading to do.

"Can we watch cartoons, Daddy?" Jamie ran for the box of Legos and dragged them out in front of the TV. "Do you like to play Legos, Mr. Bean-Man?"

Before his boys could con Wacey's poor body onto the floor, TJ shook his head. "Not now. Y'all make things and bring them to us."

"Okay!" Jamie was pretty easy, and Thomas would make one thing before drifting off with a book.

He eased Wacey down onto the sofa, then sat down beside him, close enough to feel the heat of Wacey's body. "You doing okay?" he murmured.

"I am. Tired a little, but that's no big."

"Well, take it easy, huh? Don't let them bamboozle you into anything strenuous."

"Are they strenuous, Tank?"

"They can be." He winked. "Legos can be a contact sport."

"Oh man. I don't remember that as a kid."

"I think we were better behaved." TJ snorted. "Imagine that for a moment."

"I don't believe it. These guys seem solid."

"They really are. They're good kids. They just know so much more than we did, I think." He and Wace had been teenagers at the very, very start of texting, when it was something businessmen and people from New York did. He couldn't imagine growing up with the constant stream of information his kids processed every day.

"Yeah. They have to learn so different from us." The words surprised him. Wace had always surprised him. The man was smarter than advertised.

"They do."

"Daddy, look, it's a pterodactyl!" James held up what looked like a hippo-ostrich hybrid with wings.

"Wow! I like it. Very aerodynamic."

"Aerodynamic?" James asked, and his brother, the know-it-all, snorted.

"It means it can fly, Jamie. It means you did good."

"Oh!" James beamed. "Cool." He went to toss it in the air, and Wacey caught it deftly, managing not to break it.

"I like it. Can you make a car, man?"

"I can!" Jamie stuck out his tongue and got to work.

"Nicely played," TJ whispered.

"Thank you, thank you very much."

Now who would have known Wacey Bene could do a good Elvis impersonation?

Wicked man.

TJ grinned, then winked at Tommy, who was staring a little.

"What should I make, Bean-Man?"

"A horse."

"I can do that." Tommy nodded easily, grinning a tiny bit. His grown-up boy.

"Rock on, cowboy."

TJ loved how Wace was so easy with kids. That warm smile, that Wacey not once treated them like babies.... He just loved it. Even as fucked-up as Wace was, as bad as he had to be hurting, Wace was a good man.

"You need anything, babe?" He was going to go start meatballs here in a minute.

"Just don't ask me to put my boots on right now."

"Nope. I will fetch and carry and take you to the bathroom even. You want another pair of socks to pad things?"

"Not right now. Right now I just want them to stay quiet."

"The kids?" He raised his brows.

"My feet."

"Ah." That made more sense. "Okay, you can handle these two, right? I'll be ten feet away."

"I think I can do it. If not, I will holler. You don't need help?"

"Not yet. I'll get y'all to supervise when I make the salad. They're just frozen meatballs." He was no chef, but he knew a few good gems.

"I love meatballs."

"Me too!" Tommy said. "I like them with cheese. Do you like cheese?"

Wacey grinned over. "I totally do. I like cheese and sauce."

"Garlic toast, Daddy?" Jamie didn't even look up from his Legos.

"Yes, son."

"Thank you."

Tommy handed Wacey the "horse," then came into the kitchen. "Can I read to you while you're cooking? I have three more books before I get another book to keep."

"You bet, champ. What are you reading today?"

"*Horrid Henry*. He's a bad boy. He has a brother. Perfect Peter."

"Yeah?" He doubted that meant anything philosophically, but he probed it casually. "Did you pick that for a reason?"

"Señora Martinez gave it to me. She said it would make me laugh. I like funny books."

"Me too. I like scary ones too." TJ pulled out a bag of meatballs so he could toss them in the oven.

"Do you? Which one is your favorite?" Tommy climbed up onto one of the stools at the bar, the book slapping on the counter.

"Scary?" When Tommy nodded, he pondered that. "I really like this book called *Needful Things*. It has a great cop in it, and a neat town monster. I'll give it to you when you're old enough."

"Maybe when I'm eight?"

"Maybe." He crossed his fingers behind his back. Twelve, at least. Possibly fifteen. Tommy still had nightmares when he saw the Count on *Sesame Street*. After he got through some *Goosebumps* without a hitch….

He glanced toward the front room, which was very quiet.

James was sitting in Wacey's lap, one of the man's arms draped around his littlest boy. Wacey was sound asleep and Jamie was playing quietly. When James saw him watching, one little finger lifted to his lips with a "shh."

Oh God, that was the cutest thing ever. He nodded, then winked. He went back to making dinner, confident that his boy was taking good care of Wacey.

Tommy started reading aloud, and the scent of spaghetti and meatballs and garlic bread filled the air.

God help him, he could learn to get used to this. Maybe with Wacey a little less toasted and blistered, but….

Yeah.

Still, everything that was most important to him right now was in one place. How often did TJ get to say that?

Just now.

Lord help him.

His phone rang, and he looked at it. Mike. "Yo, buddy, what's—"

"I've got your officer feller. If you don't want him to bleed out in the desert, you'd better come find him."

Shock stuttered his heart for a moment before the cop in him took over. "What? Who the fuck is this?"

Tommy's head snapped up, his mouth falling open, but TJ held up a hand to stall any words that might come out.

"I'm the man that's fixin' to ruin your life, Chief."

"Don't you hurt Mike." He turned off the stove and headed back to the bedroom to get armed. "If it's me you want, you leave him out of it."

The asshole on the other end of the line snorted. "You have no idea what I want, Chief."

"Then tell me." Keep the guy talking. Keep him giving hints as to who he was and not hurting Mike.

Wacey was standing in the bedroom doorway, watching him with a serious look.

TJ shook his head, warning Wace off. Wacey would have to stay with the kids. Shit, someone needed to call Pop Bene.

Wacey nodded, then mouthed, "Where's another piece? Don't leave me here with them unarmed."

Okay. Okay, that was fair. He tugged out the key to the gun safe, then led Wacey to the closet by the en suite, jerking his chin at it.

"I want you to get your ass out here. You want to see this cop alive again, you come alone. Mile marker sixteen."

"You hurt one of my guys, and I will hurt you where it shows."

"I'm so scared." The guy laughed, a rusty, awful sound.

"You might ought to be." He grabbed his keys and pulled the phone away from his ear, leaning down to kiss his sons. "Wacey is staying. I'll be back. I love you."

"Love you, Daddy. Be safe." Tommy looked so scared, but he was trying to be so brave. "Me and Jamie will be good."

"I know you will, buddy." He turned and left, not wanting the kids to hear any more of his conversation with this lunatic. "I'm coming for you, mister. You'd better damn well be ready."

"Kiss my ass, Chief. You know what I mean? Pucker up."

His rage grew every second. This was the man who'd tried so hard to hurt Wacey. TJ knew it, and now the bastard was coming after Mike, after him. No one was fucking safe until he got this guy.

This was his motherfucking town, dammit. And it was time for this shit to cease.

He hopped in the truck, then gunned it out of the driveway. TJ had to get out to where Wacey had appeared on the highway. And he had to do it soon.

The asshole had just hung up on him.

Chapter Eighteen

"OKAY, boyos. Let's finish making supper." The .38 was cold where it rested in the small of Wacey's back, but it was a comfort knowing it was so close. "Tommy, could you please make sure the front door is locked?"

Pop. Tank got a call and zoomed out. Lock the ranch down. Tell the girls.

Shit. Will do son.

Tommy ran to all the doors and windows and locked them. Good kid.

Jamie just sat and stared at him, face pale. "Daddy has to go be a police."

"He does. He's a hero. We'll make food. Can you help me, son? I haven't made spaghetti in a long time." He held one arm out, telling himself that he had this. He knew kids, he loved them, and these weren't just kids. These were Tank's boys.

Jamie came right to him, pressing against his side. "Daddy turned off the water. We need to boil it."

"Rock on."

"The bread goes in the toaster oven." Tommy sounded real sure about that too.

"What about the sauce, y'all?"

"Daddy has jars of Ragu."

Wacey thought somewhere his mama just exploded. Mexican or Italian, sauce did not come out of a jar. Still, he'd take it right now, the way his thoughts were racing.

"Point the way." Jesus, what the hell was going on? Who was hating on him?

I'm coming home, Dub. Fuck this shit. Just talked to Pop. I'll be there in ten hours.

He blinked at his phone, torn between telling Kace to get back and do his damn job, and cheering because him and Kace knew how to work together. Between them and TJ—

God, what if something happened to Tank? He would freak the fuck out.

Good. I need you, Bubba.

Heard. Coming. Hold down the fort.

He grinned a little, and Tommy nudged him from the side Jamie wasn't clinging to. "Who was that?"

"My little brother. He's my best friend. He's coming to the ranch to see me."

"Really? Can we meet him, Bean-Man?" Tommy moved to help him when he pulled out a bag of salad from the fridge. Tank would be starving when he got back.

"You totally can. He's a cowboy like me. He's the best."

"Wow! I want to learn that." Jamie finally let him go and hopped around the kitchen like Adriano Moraes doing a warm up.

Lord have mercy. He'd never been that… oh who the hell was he kidding? You put him and a half-dozen cowboys in a room for two hours with nothing to do and they were still just as bad.

He chuckled, relaxing a tiny bit. His tension wasn't helping the boys at all. "Ride 'em, cowboy!"

He started the water and the bread, damn near jumping out of his skin when a knock came to the door.

The boys went still, but they didn't look too scared.

"Lemme see who that is. Hold up." He put his hand to the back of his waist, then went to look out the side light.

Huh. Rusty Johnson, in full-on clown. Weird. He opened the door, keeping his hand where it was. "Hey, man. What's up? TJ's on a call."

"Your pop asked me to come out. Says there's trouble down to the ranch, and you may have your hands full."

"Oh, I'm okay." Tank must've called Pop on the way to get the gates opened.

"You sure?" Rusty edged into the doorframe. "I'm good with kids."

"Uh." He wasn't at all sure about that.

"Bean? Bean, he's a scary clown." Tommy sounded worried.

"You have your makeup on, man."

"Oh." Rusty chuckled, the sound just like his name. "Sorry."

"Bean, Jamie needs to pee." Tommy was tugging hard on his arm.

"Okay. Okay, sure. Rusty, do you mind?"

"Not at all. I'll keep an eye on that boiling water. You don't want it to boil over, do you?" And just like that, Rusty was inside.

Lord, something was off here.

"Come on, boys." The hair on the back of his neck was standing right up. He needed to get Tank's sons out of here.

Jesus, what was wrong with him? He'd known Rusty since he was a little baby. Pop'd known him even longer.

Pop.

Thanx for sending Rusty O.o

He sent the text while he herded Jamie and Thomas to the bathroom back in Tank's room. He had this urge to put the whole house between them and Rusty, sort of like when you have a dog that you've been petting every day for a year and suddenly you see foam around his mouth. Could be a toad. Could be rabies.

I didn't send him.

What?

He locked the bedroom door as quiet as he could, then knelt down to talk to Tommy while James was on the pot. "Do you and your daddy have a place that's just for y'all? A secret place to hide?"

Tommy nodded. "Yes, sir. He told me. Up in the closet attic."

"The closet attic?" What the fuck did that mean?

"Uh-huh." Tommy tugged him to the walk-in closet and pointed up to a tiny door in the ceiling. *Oh, rock on.*

"Okay. I'm going to send you up there. I want you and James to be quiet and still, and you don't come out for love or money or your daddy. Understand?"

"Yessir." Thomas was pale, but his chin was set, his expression resolute. Someone was the son of a cop.

"Okay. Quiet-quiet." How the fuck did this thing… a rope. Bless Tank. He had no jump left.

He tugged it down, and a tiny ladder popped out. Okay, he'd have to pray Rusty didn't look and see that rope if something went down badly.

Tommy went up, then Wacey grabbed James and pushed him up. Tommy grabbed the ladder and pulled. Smart boy.

They'd practiced this.

"Y'all be silent. I swear I have your backs."

Two pale little faces peered down at him.

"I swear." Then he shut the door, leaving them in the dark.

Worried about a clown. Knowing his luck, they'd be scarred for life.

He sighed, turning back to the kitchen, the comforting weight of the pistol right there. His feet were bleeding again. He could feel it.

"Sorry, man, the kids are a little wigged about the clown thing."

He damn near missed the whoosh of the bat swinging through the air, but almost missed meant that he ducked, his bad leg buckling under him for a second, and the second swing he managed to grab the wood weapon, the jolts reverberating through his arms.

Rusty pulled back on the bat, the strength in that wiry body shocking.

Still, he was forty motherfucking years younger, a hundred pounds less puffy, and he had righteous goddamn rage.

He held on. "What the fuck is wrong with you? Did you have a stroke and become a dickmonkey?"

"Me? Me? I didn't do shit and you fired me!"

Every so often, Wacey Frederico Bene could hear his mama saying to him, *"Mijo, you don't have to say everything in your head."*

This was one of those times.

"Getting fired is what happens when you don't do shit, Rusty."

"I was doing my job." Spittle flew when Rusty screamed.

"Dick jokes and fat-wife patter? Seriously? It's not 1972, man." *Pay attention, Wacey. Pay attention. He's damn near killed you now, a couple of times.* "You got a retirement. Cope. How'd you get the horses to buck? You shoot a round over their heads?"

Rusty grunted, yanking back on the bat.

He waited, biding his time. When Rusty worked up a real head of rage, Wacey would let go and the asshole would go ass over teakettle.

"You little shit. Not worth half of what your daddy is."

"Name anyone worth half of what Pop Bene is." Idiot. Like that was going to make him cry.

"You've got no idea what the rodeo is about. Your kind is ruining it!" Rusty yanked and tugged, tossing him around the room.

"My kind? You mean not ancient and used up?" Jesus, his feet hurt.

"You little fuck! You fag!" Rusty reared back so hard his feet almost left the ground, so that was when Wacey let go.

Rusty went ass over teakettle, ending up against the front door in a heap.

Wacey pulled his phone first, dialing Tank before he pulled the pistol and drew down on Rusty.

Freezing, Rusty stared at him, eyes yellow against the bright white makeup he wore.

"Wace? You okay? There's not a goddamned thing out here but Mike's fucking phone."

"He's here. Rusty. Here, man. Send the fucking Marines."

"Are the boys okay?"

"Fine as frog hair."

"Oh. Thank God. I'm on my way. I'll call dispatch. Mike might be by you. Get somewhere safe."

"I've got the fucker treed." Rusty tried to get up, and Wacey bared his teeth. "Don't you even move, you bastard."

"Jesus. Be careful. We still don't know if he's acting alone."

"Hurry up, Tank." At some point, he was going to have to shoot this bastard, and he didn't want to do that.

"I'm coming." Tank hung up on him, and he knew the man was calling in reinforcements.

Seriously? This was about his being queer? That seemed so… stupid. He'd never been in the closet, never had to be.

"Bastard. I could just bash your head in."

"You've been trying. You sort of suck at this murder game."

"Fuck you." Rusty was hard to read in his makeup, and he'd gone still, calculating his next move, Wacey'd bet.

"Seriously? You know Pop is going to beat you to death, right? How many guys are on your payroll?"

"I ain't sayin'."

So he was right. He knew it. Rusty couldn't have done it all. Not the way the setup had worked today.

"No worries. We'll ferret it out. Cut the head off and all that bullshit."

"You bastard. You stole my life."

He snorted. "I did what Pop was too close to you to do. You were outdated in the '70s."

"People love me. I'm the clown." Ranting was so not pretty, but Wacey just had to keep Rusty going until someone came.

"You're the scary clown, dude. I gave you a job."

"You took it from me." Rusty rose up to his knees, bat held at the ready.

"I didn't, and I don't want to shoot you, man, but make no mistake, I will." He refused to think about Tank's sons. If he didn't focus on them, maybe Rusty wouldn't think about them.

Rusty's eyes narrowed. "You ain't gonna shoot me, pussyman. Not with your save the animals friends and your PETA-loving bullshit."

"My…. Have you lost your goddamn mind, Rusty? Is that it? You have lost your shit in a major way?"

"I hate you." The words were low, rough, and ringing with truth unlike anything else Rusty had said. Rusty gathered himself, and Wacey knew he was going to strike.

Please, God. Please, help me. He didn't want to shoot this man, not in Tank's house.

Inspiration struck, and he shook his head. "Not here, Rusty. Not in a cop's house. You could run now. I know you got some savings. Go to Mexico." Stalling. He was stalling, and he knew it.

Rusty tilted his head to one side. "Why would you say that to me?"

"Because I've known you since I was a baby. You're rodeo, Rusty. You don't want to do this."

"I'm rodeo. Not you. You're a… traitor."

"For working my ass off? You ain't making sense." Wacey shook his head. "You saying I can't be a cowboy because I'm gay? You know that's bullshit. How many buckles did I win?"

Time ticked by so fucking slowly Wacey thought he might scream. *Come on. Someone. Anyone.*

"You threw me away like I was trash! You fired me like you had the right to do so!"

"Rusty—" The sound of tires squealing and gravel flying sounded just outside the kitchen window just about the time the water boiled over on the stove like a volcano.

Rusty jumped, turning to look, and that was all he needed. He lunged, keeping the gun up and away, and yanked the bat out of Rusty's hands. He sprang back, ready to kneecap the old fool if he had to.

"Wacey! Wacey Bene, it's Star! Star Fassbender! I'm a neighbor of TJ's, and I have a twelve gauge. Is it safe to come in?"

"It sure is. I could use some help tying up the clown."

"The clown? No shit? There's some fucking therapy there. I'm coming in." Another car pulled up, a wee sedan from the sound of it. Star came through the door, her long gray hair flying, her rainbow serape like a cape. "Ruth Ann Masters just pulled up. She shoots a nine mil at the range every week like every conservative religious nutjob." She smiled. "I hate clowns."

"I'm beginning to rethink my position too. As soon as Miz Ruth Ann comes in, can someone find the duct tape?"

"I know just where that is. Cover me, Ruth Ann."

"You got it, Starbaby."

If he'd ever been in a more surreal situation, Wacey couldn't remember it.

Rusty opened his mouth, and Ruth Ann shook her head. "I don't think so, sir. You have committed a mortal sin, and I will send you to your maker, no question."

Wacey just kept the bat in one hand and the gun in the other until Star had wrapped Rusty in enough duct tape to immobilize a bucking bull.

"You ladies have him? I got to check something." He needed to tell those boys it was under control, right? Not only that, but the pasta water was making a mess.

"We got this, Mr. Bene." Ruth Ann looked pretty competent with that Glock.

"We totally do. Go check on the boys."

He limped into the bedroom, locking the door behind him. "Boys? Your daddy's coming. Y'all can open the hatch. The bad guy's been tied up."

The door opened a wee crack. "Promise?"

"I swear to God. Y'all stay up there until your daddy comes, but you can leave the hatch open now. You guys were perfect. I'm so proud."

"We were super quiet," Thomas said.

"It's so dark." Jamie sounded snuffly.

"You were. Patience. Then we'll have supper." He had to get back out there.

"We'll stay right here. I'll keep the dark away, Jamie."

Wacey smiled. Thomas was a good brother.

"Good boys. I'll be back."

Okay. Okay, you are going back out there and dealing, and you are not going to think about letting anyone know how sore you are.

When he backtracked, he had to fight not to groan over the fact that he was leaving bloody footprints.

Señor Marin, Peter, and Josh Leman were now standing in TJ's living room, a shotgun, a slingshot, and a nail gun trained on Rusty, who was possibly the most guarded human being in New Mexico right now.

"Hola, señor, fellas. Nice to see y'all."

"Wacey." Josh gave him a nod. "I heard on the scanner and came running."

"I was talking clay with Señor Marin, here," Peter added. "He's got a shortwave. Here we are!"

Marin just winked. "The niños okay?"

"Yes, sir."

Him, not so much, but at least he had friends.

The sound of more tires on gravel made him pray it was Tank now. Or Mike. Someone who could arrest Rusty.

The door flew open, and it was Macey with a shovel. "I will beat you down for fucking with my baby brother, you fucker!"

Wow.

Wacey blinked. "Macey, it's under control. It's like a PTA meeting or something."

She glared at him. "Mama's fixin' to kill you. Just FYI."

"Kacey's coming home. She can baby him." He was way more worried about Tank's ex-wife.

Macey turned on Rusty, who stared at her, eyes wide. It was one thing, he guessed, for Wacey to see him like this, but Macey was one of the rodeo queens.

"My people were good to you. Every single one of us. You piece of shit. I swear to God, I will take my pound of flesh out of you."

He did love that, how the girls were the meanest of them all.

"Now, Macey." That was Star. "He'll get what's coming to him."

"He sure as shit will."

Josh stared at Macey like she was an avenging angel, and Wacey knew that stories were fixin' to run hot and heavy.

He managed not to roll his eyes, teetering on the verge of hysterical laughter.

Mike the cop showed up next, taking in the scene with a half grin playing around his mouth. "Well, looks like you guys have this well in hand, but I think I can take it from here now. Good job."

Well in hand.

Good job.

What the actual fuck?

One of his father's oldest friends had tried to kill him for, at best, sketchy reasons. Not just once or twice. Four times.

Four.

That seemed like overkill, to be honest.

Pun intended.

Wacey turned tail and headed to Tank's bedroom, where he locked the door, put the pistol in the bedside table, and went to fetch the two bravest little boys on earth.

Fuck this shit.

Chapter Nineteen

WHEN TJ finally got to his damned house, a whole host of people were filing out. Star Fassbender, Ruth Ann, Peter Nunn, Señor Marin….

He blinked. "Josh. Where's Wacey and my boys?"

"Bedroom. It's locked."

"What?"

"Locked. You want I should kick it down?"

"Goddamn it, Leman, you dip!" Star snapped. "I already told you now. Personally, I think Wacey Bene is a little emotionally stressed."

"You think?"

"I do. He may need tea. Or this." She slipped him a baggy with two carefully rolled joints.

"Wow. Okay." He took it, because at least that way she didn't have it. Or whatever. "Thanks."

"You need me to stay, buddy?"

"Yeah. Yeah, come on in." He felt… dazed.

He moved inside, finding Mike handcuffing Rusty the clown—who wore more duct tape than the Camaro he'd gotten when he was sixteen—with Macey Bene standing over the man with a shovel.

"Wow. Seriously?"

"Apparently." Mike didn't look happy.

"I found your phone." He tossed it over, and Mike caught it with one hand.

"Lost it at the ranch. Pop Bene said it was on the table on the porch and to pick it up after my shift. I had the radio, boss."

"I got you, man."

Mike sighed. "He hasn't given up his accomplices yet."

"Shit." TJ stared at Rusty. "You hurt Wacey, and you put my kids in danger. You might as well know I will put you away for as long as I can, old man."

"For what? Assault? I'm frail and old. You'll be lucky if I serve a day and you know it."

"Attempted murder. Wrongful death of an animal. Reckless endangerment. Criminal threat and assault of a police officer." He wanted to see his kids, damn it. "You got this, Mike? Josh?"

"I got this, boss. Go on."

"Thanks. Macey, you should go on. I'll bring Wacey out to the ranch later."

She jumped as if surprised he'd seen her. "No, Tim's got the kids. I'll clean up the kitchen and order you guys a pizza. Go."

TJ nodded in thanks and strode down the hall to knock on his bedroom door.

"Who is it?"

"Me." He waited for the door to open, finding a pale Wacey with two clinging boys in his arms.

"Hey." Relief weakened his legs, and he sagged a moment, but he knew the boys needed him to be Dad. "Did you guys do good?" He held out his arms.

"Bean says we were rock stars!" Jamie beamed, so proud, but it was his Tommy that teared up.

"Daddy."

"I got you, bud. You were so brave I bet. I know how good you protect Jamie." He hugged them both tight, and pressed a kiss to the top of Tommy's head. The sick churning in his gut began to abate.

"I did. I didn't cry, Daddy. I was brave."

Wacey nodded. "They were perfect."

"I'm so proud of you." He held them and looked up at Wacey. "You in one piece?"

"I'm fine."

He studied Wacey carefully. "You don't look it." He left it at that for now. "Who needs a glass of Sprite?"

"Me! Me!" James was on it.

"I'll grab it. In case everyone's not gone."

"Mike was taking Rusty out. Your sister and Josh are still in the kitchen." He thought it worth warning Wacey about.

"Good deal. Be right back." Wacey left them, and he scowled at the bloody footprints on the floor. Damn it.

"Daddy, is the bad clown gone?"

He nodded seriously. "He's going to jail, bud. Mike is taking him. Uncle Josh is watching."

"Bean told us to hide, and we showed him where. We were so good." Tommy's eyes were huge. "Then he comed and said we could have the door open. Then he got us out and stayed with us."

"He's a good guy, right?" He hoped the kids thought so. If Wacey stuck around at all, TJ intended them to be together. A lot.

"He's a cowboy, Daddy. They're the good guys." There was nothing but faith in Jamie's voice.

"That they are, Jamie. That they are." He would never disabuse his boy of that idea. "Miss Star came to save you too. And Miz Ruth Ann and Señor Marin. Lots of folks"

"Wow. That's cool, Daddy. Momma's going to be surprised, huh?"

"She is. Who needs the bathroom?" Monica would surely have heard by now. Shit. "I need to call Momma."

"Can we go…?"

The bedroom door opened, Wacey standing there with two plastic cups. "Y'all want to come play Legos? Miss Macey ordered pizzas, and Mister Josh wants to say hi."

"Legos!" Jamie ran off, but Thomas stayed, biting his lip.

"Bean might need you to help him, bud. His feet are real hurt."

"Oh. Yeah. I seen them. Whoa." Tommy called out, "Bean? I'll carry the drinks. Come sit with me and play?"

"You got it." Wacey limped off with Tommy, and TJ called Monica while he dug out more bandages and socks and ointment.

"You left my boys with who?"

Oh, this wasn't going to be good.

"Hey! I had no choice. The perp said he had Mike out in the desert. They like him already." Wait, was that a good thing to say?

"Oh good Lord. Are they okay? Are they scared? Do I need to come?"

"They're okay. They had to hide in their safe place, so they're a little freaked, but they're drinking

Sprite and playing Legos with Wacey and Josh." She didn't need to lose work time. She would come after, regardless.

"You're seriously hooking up with him, honey? After all this time?"

"I sure hope so." He had no idea. Now that they knew what they knew, Wacey might just recover and hit the road again. The very thought made TJ queasy.

"Well, then, I guess it's good the boys like him. Does he like them?"

"He does." TJ was still surprised how good Wacey was with kids. "He's a champ."

"He's a cowboy."

"Yeah. Yeah, that he is." And thank God for it, because when the shit hit the fan, Wacey Bene protected his kids.

"Well, I want to come now, but I have a patient I can't just leave to a short shift. I'll come as soon as I can." Monica sounded fairly relieved, though, so he'd done his job.

"We'll be here. The kids are fine. You save the world there."

"And you'll save the world there. I know."

"Wonder Twins." The joke was an old one, but she laughed anyway. "Love you."

"Love you. Go be with your sons." She hung up without a goodbye.

He tucked his phone into his pocket before gathering up all his supplies. Time to pay Wacey some attention.

Chapter Twenty

GOD, he was….

Wacey kept looking at his hands, watching them tremble so slightly that no one but him could see.

How was he going to tell his pop? What was he supposed to do now?

God, he wanted to get in his truck and drive until no one knew him, no one could see him. Just start over.

TJ had walked Josh out, Macey was still scrubbing in the kitchen, the TV was back on, the boys playing Legos, but all he could do was sit and shake.

TJ appeared from the back hall, a big wad of stuff in his hands. "Hey, babe."

"Hey there. There's pizza coming. Macey got one of the teenagers to offer to deliver."

"Cool." TJ squatted down in front of him. "I need to see your feet. I washed up in the bathroom."

"Don't worry about them. I think the socks are a loss." He didn't know exactly what to do, really. Somebody who had known him his whole life hated him enough to kill him.

"I have to worry. You bled all over my floor." TJ set the supplies aside, warm hands landing on his knees.

"I did. The pistol is in the bedside table."

"You're shaking."

"I'm trying not to."

"It happens. Adrenaline. Let me get you something to drink and all." Those dark eyes never left his.

"Yeah. It's over, huh? Or maybe not. I don't… I didn't mean to put your boys in danger."

"I know that, fool. It won't take long to find out who he was working with. I'll just call your pop." TJ's half grin made him chuckle.

"Yeah. Yeah, that's the best plan. Kace is coming home. He'll be here tomorrow."

"Well, cool." Doubt crept into TJ's expression. "You going with him when he leaves?"

He shook his head. He didn't know what to do. He just needed a minute to breathe and figure out who he was.

"Of course he is. Dub *is* that rodeo." Macey looked at him. "You look rough, Dub. You want me to take you on home? I can?"

"I—" He glanced back at TJ, who looked downright mad now. The way those eyebrows gyrated told him TJ wanted him to stay right there. The heaviness of the hands on his legs said the same thing. God help him, he was where he wanted to be. "Tell me you want me to stay and I will."

"I want you to stay, Wacey. So bad." TJ was serious. He knew this man too well to think otherwise.

"I'm good, Sister."

"But…."

"Mace. Please." He was tired and close to the edge, and there were two little boys right here.

"Right. I'll call Mama and update the house. Talk to you mañana?"

God, he loved her. For real. She came and gave him a kiss on the cheek, pile-driving TJ out of the way. "I got you meat lovers. Don't let the kids eat it all. I hear they eat healthy, so I got veggie for them."

"You rock, Sis. See you tomorrow." He patted her arm before she moved away, waving as she slipped out the door.

"Bean, can I sit on your lap?"

He wanted to cry at the thought, but he nodded and held out his arms, letting Jamie climb up into his lap. "Is this a truck you made?"

"You guessed!"

"It looks like a truck, man." Wacey grinned, even if it felt like a grimace.

TJ never said a word, just propped a pillow under his feet, then rose. "Gonna run a dishpan of hot water."

"Are you gonna do dishes, Daddy? Can I help?" Tommy went running to follow.

He heard TJ murmuring to Tommy, but he was so damned tired now, the shaking stopped. Tank had asked him to stay. Here.

"…I grow up, I'm going to be rodeo cowboy like you, Bean. I'm going to ride a buckin' bronco and wave my hat in the air…."

"Are you? You better go to rodeo school, then."

"We start next week." Jamie nodded, hair brushing his chin.

"You'll get to meet a lot of my very good friends and my folks. My little brother too."

"He's a cowboy too? That's so cool!"

"He is, I have two older sisters and a little brother. Lacey, Macey, me, and Kacey."

"Wow." He got big eyes from Jamie. "Daddy is an only, and Momma only has a sister."

"I have a big family. It's pretty cool. I spend lots of time with just my brother, though. He's my best friend." And Wacey needed to talk to Kace, needed to just talk to someone who got him, on a genetic level.

"Like me and Tommy."

"Just like that," Tank said, kneeling down in front of him again. "Tommy wants you to come help him get plates and napkins for pizza, bud."

"'Kay, Daddy!" James bounced off his legs and went running.

"Sorry about that. I know you're sore to death."

He nodded, then shrugged to hide the motion. "I'm cool. He's a good kid. They both are."

"Yeah. Thanks for taking care of them, Wace. I mean it."

"They're yours. Of course I took care of them."

TJ blinked up at him, lashes dark and heavy, eyes full of an emotion Wacey couldn't put a name to. Then TJ pushed up to kiss him right on the mouth.

Chapter Twenty-One

TJ sat back from the kiss, breathing hard.

"Daddy! You kissed Bean-Man!" Jamie stared at them, eyes wide, a bunch of silverware clutched in both hands.

"I did. I like him, a lot." And he wasn't ashamed of it either.

"Like in the movies? Where people kiss?" Jamie was too young to remember him and Monica being more than passing physical together.

"Yep. Like in the movies. Go set the table, son."

"'Kay!"

Wacey stared at him with wide eyes. "Like in the movies, huh?"

"Yep." TJ chuckled. "Monica and I divorced when he was two."

"I can't say I'm sorry, but I know you wanted it to work."

"I owed it to Monica to be truthful, though. It's better this way." He hoped. God, he hoped.

"I'm sorry about Rusty. I swear to God, I didn't know. I would never—"

"I know that, you dork." He made himself move, drawing off Wacey's socks. "Jesus, babe. You need to just go into a bubble." The poor feet were shredded, the blisters popped, the skin hanging. "I am going to clean your feet up, and you are staying off them."

"But—"

"Please, Wace. Let me love you, huh?" This wasn't some weird masochistic thing. This was caring for someone he loved.

"I never wanted anything more." Wacey looked at him like that was not at all what he intended to say.

His heart began to thud against his ribs. "I mean it, you know."

"I know. I mean it too. Assuming this whole attempted murder thing eases, we might make it work."

He bent his head, hope such a terrible thing that he couldn't bear it for a moment. He dunked Wacey's foot gently into the water, which was just hot enough and had a tiny bit of soft soap foamed in it. He had a squirt bottle to rinse with.

"Jesus, that stings."

"Daddy! The pizza's here!"

Wacey looked at him and started chuckling, the sound warm and tickled, not mean at all. "I'm good here. Honest."

"Okay. Just put your feet on the towel over the pillow, okay?" TJ climbed to his feet, grabbing his wallet on the way to the door. "Hey, Nicky. Thanks for delivering."

"Miz Macey paid already. Sue sent a six-pack and a bag of chocolate chip cookies on the house."

"Thanks so much." He tipped an extra five, because that was too damned nice. He grabbed the boxes and bags. "Tommy, come carry drinks!"

"Coming, Daddy! Is Bean coming to sit at the table?"

"No, he is not. So guess what?" He handed Thomas the six-pack of soda.

"TV trays!" Jamie scrambled to help.

"Oh… wow. We're going to sit in here?" Wacey played along. "How cool is that?"

"On the couch! I love that." Thomas beamed, grabbing all the stuff from the dining table and bringing them to the coffee table.

"Bean!" Jamie stopped, stared. "Your feets!"

"I walked a lot today, kiddo." Wacey reached for socks, but TJ stopped him.

"Let me finish up, and then we'll eat. Two minutes." TJ washed off his hands in the basin before rinsing Wacey's feet, then patting them dry. He used a blister cream, then sterile bandages in a light wrap before putting socks on those poor piggy toes. "Ta-da."

"Thanks." Wacey's cheeks were pink. "Should I stay here?"

"You should." He washed up quickly. "I have a lap tray you can use."

"Can I sit next to Bean, Daddy?"

TJ thought Jamie had a new crush.

"That okay, Wacey? Or should I make him share the love seat with Tommy?"

"It's absolutely fine. I can sit with you anytime."

"Oh, man, listen to you." He winked, but it warmed his heart, the way Wacey already treated the kids like family.

"I will sit with you, Daddy. In case the clown man comes back." Poor Tommy.

"Thank you, bud. You know how I feel about clowns." TJ had a feeling he'd passed down his clown phobia to his kids, so he tried to make light of it.

"And he won't come back, Tommy. If he does, I will take care of it. Me and your dad." Wacey sounded so sure.

"Okay." Tommy took a piece of veggie pizza, only to hand it to Jamie.

"Thank you. Bean, do you want my mushys? I don't like them."

"Sure, kiddo. You can give them to me." Wacey held out his plate to receive mushrooms, and they ate like a family. In front of the TV. With no murderers.

He could learn to like this. He really could.

He glanced at Wacey, finding Wace staring at him, not the TV.

They really had a chance to start over. TJ just hoped he didn't manage to screw it up.

Chapter Twenty-Two

"**MONICA** hates me." Wacey stared across the front room at Tank. "Like seriously."

And honestly, he didn't need anyone else hating on him. His soul was heavy.

"No, she doesn't." Tank closed the front door, then wandered back over to sit next to him. "She's just freaked out that her kids were in the same room with a killer."

"Only for about ten seconds. I moved them fast." Thank God for Pop and his texting fingers of doom.

"You did. Thank you." Tank took his hand, just holding on. "What do you need, babe?"

Monica had taken the boys, citing the need to sit up and watch them sleep. He would feel the same way about any of his family.

"I don't know." It was the most honest he could be.

"Well, I don't know why." Tank chuckled. "I could use some ice cream." Tank did love his ice cream.

"Yeah? I'll take a cookie." And a hug. He needed one of those.

"Let me get the stuff." Tank rose once more, moving to grab Cokes and ice cream and cookies. When he came back, he sat close, as if he'd heard Wacey's thoughts.

Wacey leaned in, closing his eyes against the world.

Tank put an arm around him, holding on, then kissing the top of his head. He felt the thump of Tank's heartbeat against his arm, soothing him.

"It's been one hell of a day, Tank." *And that, ladies and gentlemen, was the fucking understatement of the year.*

"It has." Tank handed him a cookie with the free hand.

He took a bite, but the sweet made him grimace. "Sorry. Guess that wasn't what I was after."

"Breathe, Wace. I got you."

"I wasn't evil to him, man. I swear to God. I fired him, sure, but he was boring the crowd at best, offending at worst. I just sent him down."

"That's your job, babe." Tank's words stirred his hair, the space between them barely enough for air.

"Then why?" Be pissed. Hell, fight him, but this? He was *broke*, for fuck's sake!

"Because he's a nutjob." The certainty in Tank's words made him laugh a little. "I mean, really. You provided him with income at the school, a secure job for the rest of his life. That's more than most barrelmen get, and you know it. Some people are just fucked-up."

"You think so, Chief?" He tried another bite of cookie, this one tasting better.

"I do. I mean, if this guy was a real cowboy, he would have just shot you and left it at that." Tank was stroking his arm, not eating ice cream.

Wacey sat there for a second, then began to laugh, the sound raw and harsh. "No, he didn't want me dead. He wanted me spoilt."

"Good thing you're not milk." TJ sobered a bit. "You'll come back from this, Wacey. Shit, you were out riding this morning."

"I was, and it felt good. It felt damn good to ride and not be trapped in the arena."

"See?" Tank squeezed him gently. "You'll make it. I'll help."

"You do." Hopefully TJ wouldn't change his mind either, when people started talking. Because they would, even in Turquoise. Hell, his folks accepted him being gay ostensibly, but how would they react if Wacey openly started taking up, or living with, a man?

Living with.

Whoa.

Could he do that? Could Tank? TJ had kids, but the boys had seen them kiss, and Tank hadn't seemed to panic. In fact, it had been the opposite. Tank had just let it be what it was. A kiss between two men in love—two people in love.

He would never have believed it if it hadn't happened. Tank was so damned easy in his skin now. So… ready.

"What are you thinking about so hard, Wace?"

"Whether people would freak if I moved in with you." The words popped out of his mouth like he'd meant to say them. Jesus, wasn't he supposed to be all laconic and shit?

"Some would, I guess. I mean, I'm out and so are you, but there's always folks who can handle the theoretical who can't take reality." Tank's body moved against Wacey's when he shrugged. "I don't really care if they burn us in effigy at the courthouse."

"They'd probably just do it on the mesa. More people would see it." Were they talking about this? Really? "What about your wife?"

"My ex-wife, honey."

"Your ex-wife. What about Monica?"

"She has a live-in boyfriend, babe. She and I have talked about it at length in the past. What if I found someone? I think she might be wigged for a bit, but only because she went to high school with you."

"Yeah, and she stole my boyfriend."

"We were young. Really young." Tank pinched his arm. "You two will love each other and gang up on me regularly."

"I hope so." Wait, had they come to some agreement somehow? There had to be more to it than that. When he'd first come back to town, they couldn't even sit in the same restaurant.

"What? You're still thinking too hard, babe. I can smell the smoke."

"Just been a long day. Pop always says not to make decisions until you've calmed down."

"Mmm." Tank let it go, which he was grateful for, because he was sinking. So tired. "You're staying the night, at least. Are you ready to go to bed, Wace? I'm pooped."

"I'm staying as long as you'll have me, and God yes. Please."

"I love it when you're babbly." Tank rose and cleaned up their snack before coming back to him, then lifting him easily off the couch.

"Tank! I can walk."

"I know that. I also know I put a ton of work into those blisters so you'll heal. Indulge me, pocket cowboy."

"I can do that." He leaned into TJ's chest. "I can do that, love."

Chapter Twenty-Three

"MORNING, Chief." Mike sat at his desk, tapping away with four fingers on his keyboard when TJ got into work the next morning.

"Hey. You get any sleep at all?"

"Not yet. Our prisoner was transferred to county this morning. He kept threatening to hurt himself. They have facilities. We have…."

"A coat closet, basically, I know."

"Yeah. I just figure they can keep an eye on him." Mike chuckled, one eyebrow lifting. "I reckon he wanted to avoid the lynching."

"You think? Christ. You hurt one Bene and you've attacked a whole town."

"Well, and the rodeo folks…." Mike waggled that same eyebrow. "They'd take him out to the desert, never to be seen again. He didn't want to set bail."

"Huh. Any news on who he might have been working with?"

"Pop Bene called and said two cowboys left yesterday, just out of the blue. I got names, but not much else."

"You put a call out on them?"

"I did. Anyone picks them up for anything, they're going down." Mike shrugged. "Looks like your guy is safe for now."

"Yeah." His brain went two directions so fast it damn near hurt. The first thought was that hopefully those men ran and that Martin and his boys didn't drive them naked into the desert. The second, and the most important, was the casual, easy "your guy."

"Anyway, Ed is coming in to take a shift. I'm gonna head home." Ed was a retired cop who was still on the part-time payroll. He kicked in and helped during the weird times, just like today.

"Good deal. I'll holler if we need you."

"Yeah, no. No calls. Sleeping." Mike rose, then stretched and yawned.

"I hear you, man. I do. I promise, only for extreme emergency." He waved Mike out of the office before heading to his desk to check his messages and emails.

It was tough to concentrate, knowing Wacey was in his bed at home. Macey was coming to get him soon, because he needed to see his family, but TJ had been over the moon to see him there first thing.

Wace had been sleeping like the dead, just as if he hadn't rested in too long.

He keyed up his emails, answered mostly by rote. No to this conference. Yes to this meeting. Man, he liked it when his job was boring.

He heard the front door open, then close, then he heard, “Hey, Monica.” *Dammit.*

“Hey, Maria. He’s in, right?”

“Yes, ma’am.”

“Good.”

Oh, were those angry footsteps? She was sure putting her feet down hard. Maybe they were just “we need to talk” footsteps and she was ramping up.

Whatever it was, he’d deal. They had a lot of experience working their shit out.

“Hey, lady. Where are the boys?”

“With Jeanie at the library.” Jeanie was Monica’s bestie from high school, and oh, she didn’t care for TJ.

“Does that mean I’m in trouble?”

She pursed her lips but handed him a bag with a Styrofoam cup of coffee and half a dozen breakfast tacos. “No. Not if you answer my questions well.”

“Ah. Torture by taco.”

“Indeed. The bean-and-potato ones are mine.”

“I did wonder. How much do I owe you?”

She plopped down across from him at his desk. “Don’t worry. I will make you pay and pay.”

“Yeah, yeah. What’s new? I had no reason to believe the kids were in danger, Mon.”

“I know. I do. But Tommy dreamed about clowns all night. I know you try not to involve them in your job, but this was scary.”

“I know.” TJ put down his coffee and took her hand. “You know my heart stopped when Wacey called me.”

She gripped his hand hard. "I know. I'm sorry I didn't stay to chat last night, but Wacey's feet…. Did you want to borrow my carpet shampooer?"

"Nah. Señor Marin has a son who does that stuff professionally. Steam clean and all."

"That was… intense. I was scared." She teared up, but the tears didn't fall.

"I'm so sorry. I had no idea he would dare to show up at my house. I thought Mike was in real trouble."

"I know. I know, and bad things can happen anywhere, but… did it have to happen the first night you had 'Bean' over?"

He chuckled. "They like that, huh? Calling him Bean-Man."

"Jamie thinks he hung the moon or held the ladder for someone that did."

"He's good with them. I was surprised, which I guess isn't fair. God knows, cowboys have babies, and he's been around them all his life." He searched her face. "Are you mad? About Wacey?"

"Are you going to get in trouble? Here, I mean?"

"At work? No. I've been very honest and I'll continue to do that. There will be grumblers, but I do a good job." He hoped that was true.

"And him? Is he going to run off and rodeo?"

"He says he's staying. I have to chance it." He had to. For the first time in years, he was looking forward not back with Wacey. He had to run with it.

"You want me to take the boys full-time for a few weeks, honey? I will."

"No. No, we'll work out our lives with the kids. Wacey has to know they're my priority."

"I bet he does." She sighed, then reached in the bag for a taco. "Kinda makes me sad, Teej. I mean, I know we both moved on, but this is the one I won you from." She winked, then took a big bite, and he knew he wasn't in trouble.

"He is, and I don't regret it. I'm a lucky guy."

"You so are. Don't forget it. Eat your breakfast, doof."

"Yes, Mother."

"Uh-huh. I totally want to be on speaker when you tell your folks about Cowboy Bene."

"Oh, God." His mom would wave the rainbow flag and then go join some UU church organization to support him. His dad would get real quiet but eventually tell him to come up for supper soon. With Wacey.

"They'll love him. Your dad is aching to get into the Bene fold."

"You think?" He might be a townie, but his dad was a cowboy all the way. Deep down and skin up.

"I know. No question." She licked her fingers. "So, have you two actually done the deed?"

"Huh?" He widened his eyes as big as he could. "Are you asking me to kiss and tell?"

"Yep. Come on, man. Dish."

"He's been too tore up for acrobatics." They'd had some orgasms, but nothing energetic.

"Too bad. How bad is he? Is he… damaged?"

"Monica! No, he's just scarred up on his one leg and sore as hell. Trust me, it all works." TJ scowled at her.

"Good! What? I know you. You like having sex!"

His cheeks heated, but she did know that and, again, not ashamed. He was damned impatient for Wacey to heal enough to ride him like a prized pony. "Well, yeah, but it's weird talking to you about sex with him."

"I know. That's why I'm asking."

"Freak. Thanks for breakfast." He grabbed a taco, which was perfect. Bacon and egg and potato.

"My pleasure. Me and Jack want to have you two over for supper once he feels better."

"Yeah?" He beamed at her. "Thanks, lady. Really. I mean it."

"Well, we are going to have to spend the next twenty years raising boys together."

"This is true." He loved that. "No one I would rather do it with."

"Also good. Eat your tacos, Teej."

"Yes, ma'am." He winked at her, feeling even better than he had when he came to work.

He might be able to survive this.

Chapter Twenty-Four

"YOU look like shit, Bro."

Wacey looked at Kace. "See if you look so good after four homicide attempts, shithead."

"Jesus, you're a whiner. Only four? At your age?" Kace winked at him, then stepped up to hug him tight. "No more, Dub. No more of this."

"Yeah. I've learned all attempted murder can teach me."

"Rusty. For fuck's sake. He used to babysit us!" Kace was so damned outraged.

"I know. You were there, Bubba, when it all happened. You know I wasn't an asshole!"

Kace snorted. "I think you were too damned nice, as much as he'd been drinking."

"I did too." He sighed. God, he wanted to go home. Like to Tank's house home. Still, he'd needed to see Kace, and Lacey had shown up this morning with walking orders to fetch the wayward Bene.

He grinned. In fact, he thought he was about to be the subject of a family meeting. He needed his shit together to handle that.

"You're on my side, right, Kace?"

"There's a not your side?" Kace blinked at him, then pushed him down on the couch and sat with him. "There is not going to be a side where you're a bad guy, man."

"No? Good." The firm belief in Kacey's voice made him happy. "How's it going on the road?"

"Good. I mean, there have been some grumblings, just like when you took over, but it's all good." Kacey raised a brow. "You're not coming back, are you?"

"Do you want me back?"

"Sure, Dub." But Kace shook his head, and Wacey wasn't sure he even knew he was doing it.

"We'll see what Pop says." Wacey knew, though. Tank had asked him to stay, and not just the night.

"Look, I want you to know, I… I'm loving this, being the boss."

"Since when?"

"Since I got the chance to do the job on my own."

"Huh. Little dictator." Wacey winked. He felt good about that, though. Kacey wanted the job for real.

"You taught me well. I'm ready, though. I'm ready to take control. I've never had more fun." Kacey turned to face him. "Seriously. It's time for me to move up."

"It's not like I'm old, man!" Was he? No! No, in fact, he was young for a roper.

"I know. But you are about to settle down and be all in one place."

"And do what?" he whispered. What was he supposed to do here in Turquoise?

"I dunno, Bro." Kacey chuckled, looking a little nervous now.

"Run the rodeo school." Derek wandered into the room, then handed out Cokes to him and Kacey.

"That's what you do, man, remember?"

"It totally is. I want to raise horses." Derek dropped that bomb as if it was nothing. Boom.

"You what?"

"I want to raise cutting horses, not babysit a bunch of cowboys. I'm not a manager. I did it for Lace, but we done talked, and you're home now."

"I am?" He was, but when had all this— "Damn, you get shot at enough, you miss all the talks."

"Yeah, well.… Macey might have had a lot of shit to say last night.…"

Wacey pursed his lips to look askance at Derek, who flushed. "So you had the meeting without me?"

Derek fastened him with a sharp look. "Dub, I been part of this family for years. You introduced me to Lace. You were my best man. Don't be any dumber than you have to be. Macey called my woman."

"Sorry. I just feel like everything is up in the air." Even his feet. He had them up on the ottoman, per Tank's orders. "If you're sitting, keep them up," Tank had said.

"Everything is." That was Pop, standing there like a tree, like the center of the earth. "Macey and Tim are on their way. Lacey's in the kitchen with Mama. Time for a prayer session. One for all of us. I got things to say."

"Okay." Shit. Shit, what if Pop had a fit about him and Tank? He didn't want to be at odds with his father, but he was fighting for Tank this time.

"We'll come to you, son. That'll be easiest. Just think, you might could go a day or two without that motherfucker trying to hurt you."

"I so could." He wiggled his toes, then grimaced.

"Dub didn't do anything wrong, Pop. I was there when he fired Rusty."

"I know, son. He had to file a report, and Rusty had to agree to stop drinking on the job. We all saw the paperwork." Pop nodded easily. "I'm not mad, boys. We got some rearranging to do, is all."

Derek nodded. "Happens sometimes, I reckon."

Somehow he thought that he was fixin' to have his life changed again. Go figure.

Chapter Twenty-Five

TJ managed to make the chicken parmesan without burning, boiling over, or having to go out on a call.

He poured him and Wacey each a glass of chianti, then set out salad and garlic toast. “Voilà.”

“Wow. This smells… amazing.” Wacey looked at him like he was a miracle worker or something.

“Thanks.” He’d used frozen chicken that was already breaded, but he felt good about the whole deal. “Makes up for the turkey meatballs.”

“Yeah. That was… something else.”

“It was.” TJ shook his head, a dull sick in his belly at the thought of his boys here with that bastard. “You sure you want to sit at the table? Your feet….”

"I'm sure. This is fine. It's great." Oh, Wace had something on his mind. TJ could see the smoke coming out of his ears.

God, what if he'd changed his mind? What if Wacey was leaving?

TJ grabbed his wine and took a big drink.

"I got to talk to you, about some serious stuff, Tank." Wace cut a bite of his chicken, staring at it.

"Okay." He twirled pasta on his fork. "Are you leaving?"

"No." The word was immediate, easy, and TJ knew that it didn't matter, whatever else it was. They'd work that shit out. "But Pop and Mama are."

"What?" His eyebrows rose to his hairline. "Where are they going?"

"They want to take the fifth wheel and travel around the country. I… Kace is taking over my position, and I'm taking over the school here." Wace looked at him, so serious. "The school and the house."

"The school and the—" TJ stopped, then took a deep breath, staring into Wacey's eyes. "So you don't want to move in with me? I mean, I know it was fast."

"I was sort of hoping you might be interested in moving in with me."

He sat back, his fork clinking against the plate. "At the ranch? For real?"

"I'm getting the main house. Kace brought my horse back. You can bring the boys' horses, of course. It'll take a month or so, for all the arrangements, but… the boys can each have their own rooms. We could maybe get them their own dog…."

TJ just sat there, and he knew he'd been quiet too long when Wacey began to squirm. "That sounds amazing. I can always rent this place out. I mean just because the market is slow in Turquoise right now."

"Sure. You could do whatever you wanted. I just… I want to… you know… be with you. Permanent. I told my folks. They said to tell you they were Papaw and Mamaw for your boys."

That choked him right up, and TJ blinked hard. "Wow. I mean. Wow, babe." He groped for Wacey's hand.

"Is that a good wow?" Wacey held on tight.

"It is. Your folks have always been kind, really, but I know they weren't my biggest fans." His world spun a little, but in the best way.

"We're a family, huh?" Wacey stared at him from across the wineglass.

"We are. I can't." He laughed out loud, joy spreading through him. "I never thought I would look forward with you, not back."

"I never thought I could come home."

He squeezed Wacey's hand, the cop in him starting to run scenarios. "We have a lot to plan. I mean, what is your mom gonna do without all her stuff?"

"The kitchen will always be a community thing, I think, but she's moving into Lacey's house. Lacey needs something bigger with the new baby, and they want to run cutting horses."

"Wow. Man, how did everyone make all these plans while we were busy keeping you alive?" He finally let go of Wacey so he could eat because his belly was rumbling.

"I blame Derek. He's apparently been itching to get out from under the school. This was his chance."

"No shit?" Still waters ran deep or whatever. "That's something. Me, living at the Bene Ranch."

"You think the boys will be okay with it?"

"They will shit themselves with joy. Hot and cold running cowboys. Unlimited access to Pop's library."

"Horses. Goats. Llamas. Chickens." Wacey lifted his glass. "Cheers, Tank."

"Cheers." Excitement had his heart pounding against his ribs. They were gonna do this. They really were. With a month or so to get to know each other again, find out things like who left wet towels on the floor and how they loaded the toilet paper on the roll….

Wacey clinked their glasses together, then drank deep.

TJ watched that tanned throat work, and his brain went right to Monica asking if they'd done the deed. Down, boy.

"You ever kissed a man right after a drink of wine, Tank?"

"Nope. Is it good?" That was not helping his heart rate.

"I hope so." Wace moved over, glass in hand, and straddled his thighs. "Let's do this."

Epilogue

"CHIEF! Chief Cook! Did you see what Star painted downtown?"

Wacey hid in his coffee cup, refusing to meet Ruth Ann's eyes. This wasn't his job. This was Tank's. He was here for breakfast and to take the boys back to the ranch once Monica dropped them off.

"I did. I think it's real pretty." Tank smiled at Ruth Ann easily, looking totally in charge.

"Are you serious?"

Oh, Lord. Wacey shot a look to his lover, who just grinned. "I am serious, Miz Ruth."

"Nonsense. This is a piece of art! This is glorious! Real pretty, my ass." Miz Ruth waved her hands in the air. "It has everything! Horses and the Virgin and flowers and the mountains!"

"Oh, well, yes. I'm glad you're pleased."

"I am. I'm taking her a basket of jellies and my homemade bread."

"You do that. She'll be tickled." TJ winked at Wacey, who hid his snort in his coffee too.

"She will. I'm sure." See him, see him be all Zen and shit.

"Oh, good. I'm so glad you convinced her to be part of the community. So much nicer now." Ruth Ann patted Tank's shoulder.

"Well, I live to serve, ma'am."

No laughing, Wacey. None. Zero. Straight-faced.

He just loved it when Tank got his humble public servant face on.

"Have a good day. Wacey." She rarely pretended he was invisible these days. How nice. Rodeo trash moved up in the world when they hooked up with the police chief.

"Miz Ruth." He nodded, since his hat lay on the seat next to him and he couldn't tip it.

She headed off, and Tank chuckled softly. "Go Star for making nice."

"Yeah.... Was Star casting spells?"

"Probably." Tank winked, then forked up more hash browns. Wacey was always amazed at how long it took Tank to actually eat when he was holding court at the diner.

"You want enchiladas for supper? Bessie's coming this afternoon to cook." They'd been having Martin's wife come over once every couple weeks to make up some dinners they could toss into the oven, mostly kid-friendly.

"Sounds fab. You know I love those. Green?" Tank adored some green chile.

"I'll have her leave that out."

"Ha-ha." Tank's boot touched his under the table.

"I'm going to take the boys out riding this afternoon, so if you can't get me on my phone, call Martin."

"What time?"

"Around two, I think."

"I might have to see if Mike will fill in for me." They went riding together a lot. Tank had a surprising amount of flexibility since crime was slow in Turquoise now that no one was trying to kill Wacey.

"I'd love that. Tommy's a natural in the saddle." Jamie would be a racer one day, but Tommy was made for his butt behind the horn.

"I know, right? Morning, Eve. What can I do for you?"

One of the horsey set had a bone to pick with one of the hippies, and it went on until the boys arrived twenty minutes later.

"Bean! Bean, I drawed you a picture!"

Wacey opened his arms for Jamie, shooting Monica a happy glance. "Hey, lady."

"Hey, Dub. How's it hanging?"

Thomas frowned. "Hanging what?"

"You know, we're hanging around." He was getting good at this. Hell, after nine months of being a half-time stepdad, he ought to be.

The boys were an absolute joy, and Wacey ended up with a whole host of his nieces and nephews about when Jamie and Thomas were staying over.

"I hate to drop the kids and run, Teej, but I have to go." Monica bent to kiss each boy, then Tank's cheek. "You guys be good. All of you."

"You missed me!" He lifted his chin for his peck on the cheek.

"You dipshit," she whispered, then pecked a kiss on his skin. "He still good in bed?"

"Amazing."

"Lucky duck." She winked broadly. "I'll come for you two on Sunday, okay?"

"We're going to have a big cookout Sunday for Lacey's birthday. You want to come? We'd love to have y'all."

"That would rock. What do I bring?"

Tank laughed. "Potato salad. Definitely."

"Please. You make the best."

How did this happen? How did Turquoise draw him back in? It just didn't make sense.

"Bean, I brought my 'port card. I got all Es. Can I have a puppy of my own now?" Lord, Tommy was as determined as his daddy.

"I dunno. Someone forgot to feed Frost last night." They'd picked up a Great Pyrenees Husky mix at the pound about six months ago. It was ridiculous how much Tank loved that dog.

"Me and Jamie were at Momma's house last night. Blame Daddy."

"Oh, hey, I was on call." Tank blinked owlishly, going for innocent. "I did give him kibble, I swear."

"Well, he tried to convince me he was starving." Wacey winked. "Your daddy and I will talk on it."

"I've been reading, and I want a Saint Bernard, okay?"

"Me too! Me too, Daddy!"

Wacey looked at his lover, grinned. "You boys need breakfast?"

"Momma gave us half an apple and peanut butter so we could eat with you and Daddy," Thomas said gravely.

"Can we split a hash browns bowl?" Jamie asked.

"Easier than a Saint Bernard," Tank murmured.

"Yeah… way easier than two."

Tank grinned at him, mouthing the words he thrilled to every damned time. "Love you."

He knew Tank meant it now, wasn't ashamed of it. Or of them.

"Love you too, Tank. Miss Jenny, can we have a bowl of papas for these two hooligans?"

"You bet, Dub." She bustled up to pour more coffee and give the boys glasses of milk.

"Chief Cook? Chief Cook, can you come down to the library?" Ana Martinez came up, looking a little panicked. "There are people protesting GMOs and scaring the children."

Wacey tuned out, examining Jamie's drawing, trying to keep from hooting. Protests at the Turquoise Municipal Library. They were descending into anarchy.

Thank God the good people of their town had Tank to protect them. Even better, no matter what happened during the day, Wacey knew who TJ Cook was coming home to at night.

Coming in April 2018

DREAMSPUN DESIRES

Dreamspun Desires #55
Sweet Nothings by T. Nielson

Will a bitter bite from the past spoil a sweet romance?

Tristan Love, the youngest of seven brothers, is back in his hometown. He's left the New York food scene and an abusive relationship behind him, but he holds his love of French pastries close to his heart and is determined to put his skills to use in a bakery of his own.

Returning to his childhood home means his meddlesome brother Simon will butt into his business, but before the bakery even opens its doors, Tristan's delectable creations have the town's mouths watering, and Jake, a cute mechanic, asks Tristan out. It all seems worthwhile….

That is, until the bakery burns down, Jake's criminal past comes to light, and Tristan's nasty ex rears his head where he is decidedly not wanted.

Dreamspun Desires #56
A Full Plate by Kim Fielding

Opposites come together for a spicy surprise.

Bradford "Tully" Tolliver has everything—money, a great car, a beautiful condo, and a promising career as one of Portland's hottest young lawyers. Sure, he puts in long hours and has no social life to speak of, but who needs romance when corporations pay top dollar for his expertise? He hesitates when a colleague asks if her cousin can live with him, but the arrangement will last less than a year, and then the cousin—Sage Filling—will return to his tiny hometown.

But Sage is handsome and intriguing, and his cooking makes Tully swoon. Sage has obligations back home, though, and Tully has offers he might not refuse from a persistent—and very wealthy—ex. Since Tully and Sage each have a full plate, can they make room for a side of love?

Now Available

DREAMSPUN DESIRES

Dreamspun Desires #51
Swann's Revenge by Shira Anthony

Can a swan make peace with his ugly duckling past?

Chubby geek Jimmy Zebulon's heart broke the day his high school crush, Danny Parker, did nothing as his teammates tormented Jimmy. Fifteen years later, Jimmy is long gone, and from his ashes has risen Robert Swann, successful owner of a law firm with movie-star good looks. Robert thinks Jimmy and his past are long forgotten—until attorney Dan Parker shows up for his first day of work at Rob's firm.

An injury playing college football was the best thing to ever happen to Dan. It turned his future in a better direction—and allowed him to finally emerge from the closet he hated being trapped in at school.

Dan and Rob are immediately drawn to each other, but Rob can't bring himself to tell Dan who he really is—and their pasts might ruin any chance for a future filled with love.

Dreamspun Desires #52
Teaching Ben by Shae Connor

Learning to love means a study in patience.

Fresh out of the military, Ben Cooper is ready for a new start. He's away from his domineering father, making his own choices… and out of the closet. On his first day of college, he meets David Powell, who's just the kind of gorgeous man Ben's dreamed of. Too bad David's his teaching assistant—which makes him off-limits in Ben's eyes.

David is Ben's age, but his path couldn't be more different. He's close with his family, who helped him deal with personal struggles after he came out. He's staying away from any hint of scandal, but Ben's a kind of temptation he hasn't faced in years. If only Ben wasn't his student.

As the semester progresses, and their lives become more entwined, and keeping their relationship platonic becomes more difficult. They just have to hold out until the end of term….

FOR
MORE
OF THE
BEST
GAY
ROMANCE
DREAMSPINNER
PRESS
dreamspinnerpress.com